THE WORLD'S BIGGEST LIE

Shape of the Earth

Eric Alan Soldal

A Novel

The World's Biggest Lie: *"Shape of the Earth" a Novel.*
Most names are fictitious or changed for privacy and protection.
Scriptures are taken from the Holy Bible, KJV. This is a work of
fiction, from an historical and Biblical perspective.

Published in the United States of America. 2024.

1st Edition

ISBN- 978-1-7356254-5-4

Cover Design By: Courtney Artiste, with Elisabeth Soldal

Author Contact information:
Website: www.faithonfire.net
Email: ericsoldahl@gmail.com

Dovestar Publishing International
7149 Highway 11 Box #42 Sunset, SC 29685-9998

Dovestar Publishing International

Dedication

This Book is dedicated to my Savior, Jesus Christ.
The story, with its parallels to our own lives, is also dedicated to my devoted wife, Elisabeth, who trusts in the Lord with all of her heart. She believes in ALL of the Bible.

Acknowledgements

With deep love and gratitude for editing and Spirit led input, from my amazing wife, Elisabeth Soldahl; for encouragement, fasting, and prayers.

Much appreciation to so many folks who directly or indirectly inspired me to write this Novel; all those level-headed 'Watchmen on the Wall,' such as Rob Skiba, Daniel Valles, Nathan Roberts, The Founded Earth Brothers, *Origins* and *The World Upside Down* film creator. Eric Dubay, for paving the way. And kudos to the guy from Great Britain sharing two hundred scriptures, who ends each one saying, "That's because it's Flat…"
With special thanks to Courtney Artiste, for Cover and assistance. To author, Caryl McAdoo, for the amazing revisions. With Blessings to Parents, Sons, Daughters, Family, Friends and Faithful Ministers. With all Glory to our one true Creator of Heaven and Earth!

Preface

Who knew?

Certainly not the many science teachers Nathan encountered over his years in the educational system; they didn't have a clue. Now in his first year at U.C.L.A., his physics professor remained blinded even after being presented with the factual truths.

His instructor responded to his well-written essay with an unwarranted diatribe, lambasting him in front of all within earshot, profanity included. A poor grade would surely follow.

As a born-again believer, he responded with a cordial email to his professor and attached an irrefutable video of the scientific facts about God's true Biblical creation. Though he hoped it would garner extra credit, it went unanswered.

The paper was returned with a giant red circled "F" at the top next to one word: *"False!"* Something compelled Nathan to write *Expose the Lies and Open Eyes*. He wanted to make a difference.

He hoped to reveal the truth to the unwary, those living in a polluted world with a false globe model. That's why he even enrolled in a secular school in the first place.

It helped that much of his way was paid by a math scholarship.

As a young boy, Nathan once asked the right question to his father, after watching a replay of the first moon landing:

"Who's filming this, Daddy?"

"Filming what, son?"

"The landing—the takeoff…"

His father, years later, confessed pondering the question and wondering himself. Who was filming it?

He still remembered watching the PBS Documentary on the Apollo Missions with his dad and grandfather on a small black and white TV. The summer of 1969 when Astronaut Neil Armstrong, sounding rehearsed through the static, stepped onto a shadowed lunar surface and spoke those famous words.

"One small step for man, one giant leap for mankind."

Grandpa laughed during the whole documentary. "Ask your science teacher how President Nixon was able to talk to those Astronauts way out there in space over a landline phone from the White House, Boy."

"Now that you mention it, Pops, how do you suppose that flag is waving in the wind when there was ostensibly no atmosphere on the moon."

Now outside the college classroom, Nathan responded to a group of mockers. "What are you—some kind of Flat Earth nut?"

"It's Biblical." He shrugged. "And scientific, too. Knowing the truth will set you free. It's for anyone with open eyes."

Grabbing an iPad with a large screen out of his backpack, an image appeared with a dozen different composites of the earth. He held it high for the group of clamoring students.

"These are supposedly images of the earth from space, but they're all faked by NASA. Photoshopped. Look at them. Really look."

An image of a young man working at the Space Agency appeared in the video. "It is photoshopped; it has to be." Nathan slid a finger over the iPad screen to reveal another photo of a grey tombstone.

"What's that supposed to be?" a student asked smugly.

"It's the grave of a Nazi scientist named Werner Von Braun, NASA's first chief. Before he died, he asked for one Bible verse to be engraved on his tombstone.

It read, '*The Heavens declare the glory of God, and the firmament sheweth His handiwork.*'

"If you care to look that up, it's Psalms nineteen, one."

Chapter One

"It is He that sitteth upon the circle of the earth, and the inhabitants thereof are as grasshoppers; that stretcheth out the heavens as a curtain, and spreadeth them out as a tent to dwell in."   Isaiah 40:22 KJV

Living in Manhattan had been quite an adjustment for Gwen Sharpe, a small-town gal at heart. Rising quickly to her new anchor post in a midsize market delighted her.

At last! Breaking into the big time.

Hard to believe it was all due to one story she reported on an ex-president involved in a secret relationship with an employee. A chef, who had died mysteriously near the Martha's Vineyard mansion owned by the former president.

Oh, his handlers successfully directed both the cover-up of the investigation and subsequent media silence that followed. Eyewitnesses claimed the Secret Service played a part of the incident.

Local police were used for misdirection, but Gwen had blasted through the lies, and as soon as her story broke, it rocketed across the face of the earth.

With such notoriety, the head of the network himself gave her the new assignment to investigate an elite group meeting in Europe. An all-points summit in Belgium on climate change under the motto: *"Save the Planet at all costs."*

Her bureau chief, a larger balding man prone to wearing white shirts and a loose tie—it always hit the floor by days end—ran a tight ship. No one dared leave the newsroom without permission until that tie hit the ground.

During the meetings in Europe, hearing the callus conversations regarding how mankind was expendable horrified Gwen. How could they refer to the masses as *Useless Eaters* and *Carbon Polluters?*

One reporter pulled her aside. "They're taking farmers lands worldwide. Their goal is 'No Farmers—No Food.'"

A transhuman undercurrent fueled many of the lectures and discussions from the speakers of the agenda. She soon discovered the two British scientists, who first promoted a so-called "climate change" were puppets of former Vice President, Al Gore and the Globalists.

Gore had made buckets of money, traveling the world promoting *An Inconvenient Truth,* a best-selling book and film. The only problem? There was not a shred of truth to the claims. On tour, Gore's roaring windpipes were cut short after a masseuse sued him for allegedly molesting her.

Those two scientists who invented "global warming" and "climate change" retracted their erroneous research, after it was revealed most all of their data had been falsified.

They had been on the former Vice President's payroll all along. In recent times, a Globalist agenda had emerged with the world's elite, embracing the ideas to seize dominant control.

In Belgium at the Climate Summit though, a stiff opposition met Gwen after she questioned the narrative.

One European leader stood on the stage, pointing a finger in her direction. "Beware these anti-climate disruptors!"

After this man's rant, they locked her out of interviewing the inner elite circle, but on the final night in Belgium, one insider slipped Gwen a note.

> **You are on the right track. There are several organizations banding together. Their secret agenda is to control the world's governments. They pollute people and lie about the earth. Depopulationists—that's what they're called. The climate narrative is only a tool.**

Wow. To hear the world's NWO elite would spew a false narrative for control and financial gain greatly disturbed Gwen. How could the top leaders promote altering and even ending humanity? Or even think of slating transhumans to become rulers?

Wasn't it Biblical? Iron and Clay would not mix.

In the hotel elevator, she overheard several younger WEF leaders discussing how those who opposed the climate agenda, Health Pass, or Central Digital Banking system being implemented would be the first scheduled for elimination.

Entering her new hotel room, it unnerved her when the door opened automatically. Maybe a scanner read the conference lanyard around her neck?

Later, writing her news report, she re-read the entire note from the anonymous official. Hmm. It mentioned the perpetrators of the false narrative sprayed the skies with chemtrails to pollute and poison the earth.

She discovered there was a pharmaceutical connection. The same men also developed bioweapons and drugs, planning to turn humans into GMOs, to destroy all flesh.

It sounded ludicrous.

Before closing her laptop, Gwen made a final entry: Why does such a large majority believe in climate change?

Something her brother had said in his last letter came to mind. Nathan wanted her to research the shape of the earth. He called it "the true domed shape." Start with the Book of Genesis, he'd told her, adding, it holds the answers.

She hoped college would straighten him out, but it didn't appear to be having any such effect. She opened the drawer of the side table. No Bible. How sad. It didn't surprise her though.

Opening the Bible app on her phone, she sighed. It'd have to do even though they had changed or deleted many scriptures. Maybe they hadn't messed with Genesis too much.

She'd placate her brother so she could say she had read Genesis. All she really wanted to do at that point was get back to New York.

On her return to the Media Network Group, in a group setting, her boss held up her scathing report to the newsroom. "This is a no-go!" He appeared to be seething. He glared at her.

"Gwen, what are you thinking? This report makes it look like the climate summit leaders are behind polluting the world!"

"I believe they are, sir. You should have heard them. Would you have me write lies? Condone their actions?"

He ignored her and went on with his meeting, but afterwards, pulled her aside. "Don't you realize we'll be tossed out of our jobs if I allow this story to break?" He adopted a somber tone.

"Do you know who owns this company?"

"Oh, please, Roger." She left to go to her desk and process it all. Her thoughts were shortly interrupted.

"Here's our new conspiracy gal!" One of the other female anchors standing by had seemed jealous of Gwen since she exposed the ex-president's affair with the chef.

The woman snickered as she passed by the newsroom. Why would she say such a thing in front of the broadcast staff? Did the lady think she was after her job or something?

Some wise words her grandmother once told her came to mind. 'Avoid foolish contentions especially from the catcallers in life.'

A naturalist, Gwen skipped bleaching her hair and the heavy makeup, avoiding the network's professional 'makeup artist.' Unlike so many others, she kept her long chestnut hair and got plenty of compliments.

So, it hurt her heart when Roger shelved her true news story on the summit in favor of an edited to the hilt fluff piece. She hated that it aired worldwide on the network.

After all their editing, it sounded as if those heads of state and the newly crowned King of England met in Belgium to save the world and were oh so concerned over the violent emerging weather patterns.

Roger called her in and handed her a new assignment, to interview the relative of a Hollywood film director who died mysteriously years earlier. New information on a possible motive had recently surfaced.

"It's perfect for you, but you'll need to hurry to catch your flight."

"Where am I going this time?"

"LA. Listen." He leaned in and lowered his voice. "In light of your new conspiracy expertise, someone upstirs is concerned about your alternative theories. Just play it straight, will you?" He chuckled, handing her the file.

"So, who is this guy?"

"Well, Stanley Kubrick, the director, died several years ago. He's the guy you're investigating. A relative called, rambling on about a final video his uncle made where he admits to filming the biggest faked event of all time."

"What's that?"

"Well." Her boss looked around before continuing. "It's plausible they would have killed him if he threatened to reveal his filming was a forgery. He evidently kept his secret for fifty years."

"That's a long time."

"Yep. Story is, his conscience got the best of him, so he confessed the whole thing to this nephew before he died—shall we say, from questionable circumstances?"

"What is it? What's the story?"

"The guy refused to reveal the cover-up over the phone. Might just be a wild goose chase, but Kubrick held regard among his peers. He's considered one of the best directors of all time, you know."

"He won a couple of Oscars or Golden Globes, didn't he?"

"Yes, he did for his classics like *The Shining* and *2001, A Space Odyssey.*"

"When do I leave?"

"Tomorrow morning, nine o'clock. Remember there's a three-hour time difference, so the interview is scheduled for four. You'll meet at the Beverly Wilshire Hotel. A Bungalow there."

"Will this guy be alone? Will I be safe?"

"Yes—but listen—he did mention that a rogue government agency or three, maybe even the Masons, might be after him, so be careful. Be aware."

"I will."

"He also thinks they most likely killed his uncle over one of his last films, *Eyes Wide Shut* with Tom Cruise and Nicole Kidman."

"I've heard of it."

Roger searched his phone. "The man sounded urgent, Gwen, Be careful. You never know in this business."

"What are you looking for?"

"The QR code for your flight." He looked up at her. "Call me from the bungalow and leave your cell turned on during the meeting. I want to make sure you're okay." His voice trailed off, and he waved her out of his spacious office.

Restless at bedtime, alone in her studio apartment, an apprehension settled over her, but even if the meeting was a bust, she'd be able to visit her little brother. Hard to believe Nathan was a freshman at U.C.L.A, well, not so little anymore.

She'd have to start saying younger instead.

That same night across the country, while his sister unknowingly wrestled in her sleep, Nathan kept finding more Bible verses on the true shape of the earth.

How could so many have missed them all those years? His eyes were getting so heavy. Dozing off, he counted verses instead of sheep . . .

Over two hundred.

A final prayer on his lips, he succumbed.

"Lord, show me your glory."

Late in the night, he awoke in his dorm with a vision etched clearly in memory. He hovered over the earth that stretched out far and wide beneath him. Nearing the top of a translucent dome that seemed alive, the manifest presence of the Lord seemed right above him.

In his mind there a voice spoke that sounded like many waters.

"Look down upon the earth, my son. What do you see?"

Nathan tried to respond . . . in awe . . . it was . . . hard to form words. Gazing upon clouds, lands, seas, and a cavalcade of colors, a bright metallic object suddenly ascended rapidly towards him.

Nathan hovered over the earth. A large bird; stationary.

"What do you see?" the voice of ages echoed.

The metallic object a bright silver suit. Menacing. Weathered and yet imposing with a glare hard to look at directly. Slowly, the bright metallic orb came closer.

"A . . . robot? Is it a giant robot of destruction?" Instantly, the spherical object began to open from the top revealing something withered inside. An old has-been. A wormlike creature, masquerading as something ominous.

The voice thundered. *"Behold the enemy of man."*

Nathan's mind flooded with thoughts and images. A flash of bright light, a serpent, a dragon, and then the worn worm. What did it mean?

Sitting up in bed with a start, his Bible fell to the floor. Peering over the side with a small flashlight, Nathan knew the pages had fallen open for him to read a specific verse:

"And the great dragon was cast out, that old serpent, called the devil and satan, which deceiveth the whole world: he was cast out into the earth and his angels were cast out with him." Revelation 12:9:

Contemplating the vision in the darkness, Nathan's insides warmed with understanding. The Lord Most High wanted him to reveal a worm that blinds the world. What an awesome blessing to be lifted up and see from above the vast level plane of the earth.

As if radiating with the knowledge of an omniscient God Who spoke to him, he was humbled and excited at the same time. The Lord wanted him to share His True Creation . . . the true shape of the earth, for such a time as this.

Why is this so important to You, All-mighty, Everlasting, and Righteous King of Kings? Why?

The answer came in a flash.

"Because I created the heaven and the earth... My real children want the truth."

Then Nathan heard one word on a light breeze: *'Believe.'*

Reclining on his pillow, he considered how believers had come to the recent realization that evolution was a deception. That a literal Genesis creation was true, but they wanted to marry an erroneous heliocentric theory as a false narrative.

A big-bang theory and six-day creation model does NOT co-exist!

"Oh, Dear Lord, thanks for counting me worthy. I could really use a faithful like-minded mentor in this worldly university."

Again, the Lord acted fast.

Later that morning, in one of the university's breakfast spots, Nathan jotted down notes in a binder:

Heliocentrism:

1. They want you to believe we are on a rotating ball spinning on an axis at approximately 1025 miles per hour—somewhat less at the supposed poles.

2. They want you to believe that the earth is revolving around the sun at a speed of 66,600 miles per hour—and the curve of the earth is .666 ft/mile squared (666 - the number of the Anti-Christ).

3. They want you to believe that our solar system

is rotating around the Milky Way galaxy at a mean velocity of 420,000 miles per hour, while the milky way itself is ripping through the galaxy at a trajectory of 2,237,000 miles per hour. A vast expanding universe with billions and billions of other stars, suns, moons, and planets.

Nathan continued the stream of thoughts, furiously writing in his notebook.

Why is it, we are traveling over two million miles per hour, yet feel nothing? No movement. We close our eyes in a quiet place and it's motionless. We're stationary.

Why is it we see the same stars and constellations in the same pattern night after night? They have revolved the same way in the firmament above since the dawn of time.

The constellation of Orion is visible at all times from the midpoint of the earth. The same latitude of the great pyramids of Egypt and elsewhere. That's impossible on a spinning orb. Water does not stick to a spinning ball either.

But gravity explains everything away, right?

No! We have to remember that the theory of 'gravity' is just that—a theory. Gravity is easy to dispute, riddled with holes! It isn't a fact.

Buoyance and density better explain falling objects. Otherwise, butterflies and bees would stick to the ground, right?

How can there be lengthy level planes on a spherical object?

These planes, or level surface areas, span for hundreds of miles without curvature over the earth.

Complex mathematical calculations flowed quickly onto the page substantiating each point from his pencil.

> Objects fall at 9.767m/s² and not 9.8m/s² What about the acceleration of those objects? Science measures it at 9.8m/s² in tests.
>
> Therefore, the centrifugal acceleration measured is zero, and there is no rotation. No globe earth. Why is it? Why? Because we live on a plane, not a planet.

Peering over his shoulder, a taller man with blonde hair and a close-cropped beard leaned in asking quietly, "Did you come up with these calculations and theories on your own, or are they published somewhere?"

"No, sir, not published. They're mine. The ideas and earth calculations, I mean."

"Apologize for eavesdropping, but as a professor of mathematics, I noted your quick calculations." Grabbing a chair next to him, the man flipped it around and sat, chair backwards. He extended a hand.

"Thompsen—Dr. Thompsen. It's a pleasure to meet you, young man."

He shook the professor's hand. "I'm Nathan. It's my first year here, first month even."

"How's it going?

"Not too well, yet. No friends really, and my science professor hates me already. He berated me in front of class for these ideas," He tapped his notebook.

"Doctor Killagrew, I presume. Some call him Doctor Killjoy."

Nathan chuckled. The moniker suited the angry professor. "Haven't heard that one."

"You will. Listen, I'm off to class, but why don't you stop by my office, or audit a class sometime. I'm upper division, however there might be a spot for you in one of my upcoming symposiums."

The professor rose and turned but spun back around. "I'm a believer too, Nathan. You're not alone here. I may be the only professor left in the department who believes God and not Darwin."

With that he made haste.

Nathan sat dumbfounded.

How did he know?

Before closing the notebook, he made one final entry.

> But isn't a lie still a lie even if everyone believes it? And the truth is always the truth, even if no one believes it!

That night, he created a graphic about hiding the Creator and the lie behind it all.

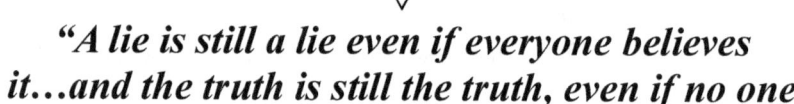

"A lie is still a lie even if everyone believes it...and the truth is still the truth, even if no one believes it."

Chapter Two

"The world also is established, that it cannot be moved."
Psalm 93:1

Elated for the first time since coming out west from Virginia, Nathan rejoiced in discovering a Level Earth group existed that met in Westwood near his campus. A well-known—at least to him—Brazilian man would be the guest speaker Friday evening.

He could hardly wait. Perhaps the most prominent of South America's Level Earthers, the PHD Physicist from the University of Sao Paulo, Alfonso de Vasconcelos, was a man he'd always hoped to meet.

What a blessing the physicist had moved to the United States. With his influence, a community of Level Earth believers quickly grew. Vasconcelos hosted a channel called "True Science," *Ciencia de Verdade.* Over a million people watched on a regular basis.

In his dark dorm room, Nathan donned headphones and watched one of those programs on his computer. So many scientific facts were presented, keeping up with his note taking wasn't easy, and with each the professor gave in-depth explanations that supported the enclosed Level Earth theory.

He stopped the video often to jot down the video links provided that exposed NASA's fraudulent program contrived decades ago to deceive the public and many in government.

Billions of tax dollars had been diverted for covert operations worldwide. They formed many fake Flat Earth narratives and societies to confuse the truth. The idea that a Flat Earth with edges floated endlessly in a vast vacuum of space, or that a Flat Earth did not exist.

"The true stationary Level Earth is historical."

Hearing the famous physicist declare this truth warmed Nathan's heart.

"There are now over twelve million people in Brazil alone who believe the stationary earth dome model. In many areas, it is taught in schools."

In the video, Professor Vasconcelos held up a domed shape earth model used in his country's classrooms, just as the spinning globes in the States' schools.

The dome he spoke of was really the firmament of the Bible. All the scientific-based professor needed was to understand the truth presented in the Biblical doctrine.

Nathan was moved to email Dr. Vasconcelos: The domed earth truth you share lines up with the Bible. Jesus reveals all truth, who is the Truth. He says, *"I Am the way, the Truth, and the Life, and no man comes to the Father but by me."*

Departing the plane at LAX, Gwen caught the pilot's eye. His crew temporarily distracted with the line of passengers disembarking, she took the liberty to speak with him.

"Thanks for a smooth flight, Captain." She smiled. "As a reporter, I was wondering about something I read recently and thought you could probably help me understand."

"I can try. What is it?"

"Well, is it true the flight manuals used during pilot training teach using a level horizon?"

"A very interesting question. What makes you ask?"

One female flight attendant moved in and stood next to the captain. "You look so familiar." She thought only a minute. "Haven't I seen you on the news? You're that reporter who exposed the president's affair with his dead chef, aren't you?"

"Ex-president." Gwen grinned at the stewardess and faced the pilot again. "You see, my brother sent me a report called *The Circle of Earth Investigation,* and it just made me wonder. So . . . if your plane's nose stays level to the earth. How is that possible with such a curvature?"

"My training was a long time ago, Miss."

"Gwen Sharpe. I apologize for not introducing myself."

"Good to meet you. We often update with flight simulators." He dodged her question.

The flight attendant spoke up. "I've wondered the same, Captain. Like over Kansas today, it appeared we could see all the way to the Rocky Mountains, right? How is that possible?"

She glanced at Gwen with a twinkle in her eye that gave the impression she enjoyed watching the pilot squirm. To make an ally, Gwen rescued the man.

"I've heard about seeing those long distances, but that would only be possible on a level plane, not a planet." She glanced again at the woman. "Anyway, that's what my brother at U.C.L.A. says."

Surprisingly, the pilot nodded making a large sweeping gesture with his arm circling in a level motion with his hand lying flat. "So then, you know."

That's all he offered.

The only passenger left, she smiled reaching for the pilot's hand, she squeezed a little. "Thank you so much, sir!"

His words stuck with her . . . *So then, you know.*

Waiting outside the baggage area a young man in a black cap held up a sign with her name: *Welcome Gwen Sharpe.*

She was a Benton but used her mother's maiden name as her reporter's pseudonym. A bit of sage advice adhered to from an older journalist in D.C. who served as her mentor at her university in Georgetown.

Her driver wove through the myriad of morning traffic, around the numerous loops that comprised the infamous L.A. freeways. He pulled in front of the Beverly Wilshire in no time. A bellhop greeted her and helped her with her bags.

It struck her as a little strange for everything to appear so well orchestrated. Even before entering the lobby, another young woman in a bright white outfit drove up in a golfcart.

"Gwen!" The young lady acted as if she knew her. "Gwen Sharpe with the *Daily Expose, right? It is you, isn't it?*"

She'd pronounced the word *Expo-Saayy.*

A moment later, they were winding through the lush grounds and pathways adorned with exotic flowers along the small cobblestone drive between the ornate bungalows.

"Here we are." The woman braked and stopped the cart. "Number 19." She hopped out and even knocked on the door for Gwen. It was weird, and she was apprehensive.

He explicitly mentioned no cameras—she recalled her boss's words. A balding, middle-aged man opened the door. "Call me Chuck." The rotund man dressed in a tunic moved to the side and motioned her forward.

She stepped inside to darkness.

A woman leisurely lay on a chaise lounge in the sun out back on a garden patio. Spotting Gwen, she reached for a cover-up. It made her less anxious, knowing another woman was nearby.

"My wife." He smiled, glancing in her direction. "Have a seat on the sofa if you will. Would you like a glass of iced tea with lemon? It's herbal." He said herbal with emphasis.

"Yes, please. That would be nice."

He wasted no time and handed her several NASA photos, then kept on talking while pouring the tea in the small kitchenette.

"These images are of the fake moon landing. They show tell-tale signs of some crude compositing and retouching. The use of studio lighting, stage backdrops, scale models, and the like, too—Scotchlite screens and chroma-keying.

"Such trickery alone represents only a small fraction of an ever-growing body of evidence proving 'The Thirty Billion Dollar $cam' funded by the taxpayer." He handed her a glass that she sipped then set on the side table.

"Thank you." Gwen processed what the man had stated, writing it furiously in her notepad. "So, Stanley Kubrick was your uncle? The famous film director?"

"More my father-in-law and boss. I worked for him many years, and my wife was considered his adopted daughter." The man glanced again towards the patio. "She thinks this interview is a bad idea."

"Why?"

"Certain people would stop at nothing to keep this information from getting out. Your bureau chief assured us the meeting will be anonymous."

"Yes, sir. Of course."

Chuck handed her a bright orange folder. "Take a look for yourself." Under the heavy weight of it, she used both hands to steady the contents.

"There's a video player inside. Keep it. Play it only when

you are in a safe place, away from anyone, and turn off every electronic device in the room, including your phone and any routers."

Glancing inside the folder, Gwen scanned the first page with highlights of its contents appearing randomly.

Stanley Kubrick CONFESSION: "I was involved in fraud. I was the movie director of THE FAKE MOON LANDING.

The CIA orchestrated footage was filmed in the desert outside of Hollywood." Telling words jumped off the page:
Few know that Kubrick's next film to be directed, was going to be 911 and he tries to tell you in all his movies about the fake moon landing film they used to deceive the whole world. His famous film 2001: A Space Odyssey, was shot about the same time.

From the day of Stanley's death to September 11, 2001 was 666 days. His last film with Tom Cruise and Nicole Kidman was *Eyes Wide Shut* that exposed the Luciferian Masonic elite, the wealthiest families, the Illuminati who really run the world.

In the end, twenty-six minutes of the film were edited out of the film against his reported last known words: "My contract gives me full creative control, and no one will change a thing as long as I live!" Kubrick was mysteriously found dead three days later.

Gwen had barely sipped on her herbal iced tea, before having her interview cut off.

"Sorry to be abrupt, Miss Sharpe, but you have all you need, and we must get going."

Walking to the rounded wooden door, he gestured her to follow then held it open for her.

"Listen, this may be the world's biggest lie. At least in the last few centuries, and it's being used by the most powerful people in the world for sheer evil. This file is all we have. It's in your capable hands now. Be careful."

"Is there a time for us to continue this interview later?" A girl could hope.

"Afraid not. This is all we've got."

His wife hovered by the back French doors. "Or all we intend to say about it. We want to honor my father's memory. Please see that you do."

Joining her husband, she handed Gwen her satchel. "Thank you for coming."

The door closed behind her. No golfcart shuttle waited out front to pick her up.

After a few weeks, Nathan mustered the resolve to drop by Professor Thompsen's office.

"Mister Benton! Good to see you. I hoped you'd stop by." The professor gestured him to sit. This Saturday morning, I'd like you to attend a special meeting we are having right off campus at Acres Hall."

"Awesome. What kind of meeting?"

As he explained the nature of the symposium, a knowing came over Nathan. It had to be a divine hand calling him inside the circle. Doctor Thompsen handed him a pamphlet.

Why do they Lie about the Age of the Earth?

Professor Thompsen, a mathematician assigned to teaching upper division classes, on his own time, had arranged to teach *The Mathematics of Creation* to a select group of students.

The private symposiums—or weekend extra-credit classes as he referred to them—were presented off-campus and without ridicule from the atheists running the science department.

"Those I've hand-picked can be trusted to keep the truth I hold sacred secure from opposition. It's a group of bright, talented students from diverse backgrounds and locations."

What an honor to be included. "I'd love to come."

That weekend, he attended his first symposium. The main topic of that week was creation versus evolution. Using numerous Biblical references, Doctor Thompsen led the discussion based also on scientific facts.

Then, by using mathematics, he seemed to confirm a young earth. A documentary segment from *Is Genesis History* was shown before the class ended.

Exiting the hall, Nathan sidled up next to Professor Thompsen.

"Well? What did you take away from this morning's lesson?"

"I loved how the age of the earth can be proven—it being young—scientifically. Adding in the Scriptural references.. I enjoyed it very much, sir. It's great to know others believe as I do."

"Believe in creation over evolution, right?"

"Yes, sir, but . . . Well, maybe the bigger picture is not being considered here."

Just then two other students interrupted the conversation, distracting Dr. Thompsen.

Turning to leave, Nathan reached into his pocket and retrieved a flyer he'd made in response to the one for the symposium the professor had given him.

Its title: *Why do they lie about the SHAPE of the Earth?*

Handing it to Dr. Thompsen, he nodded and left. Walking back to campus, Nathan became even more resolute about attending the *Level Earth Group* meeting the following night.

That next evening in the lobby of the meeting hall off campus, students posted photos of the earth by NASA. They lined the walls. Stickers were placed over them, with the saying: *'Photoshopped'*

But they had to be, didn't they?

Many different representations of a 'globe' earth had been released by NASA over the years. Each one proved completely different from all the rest, including the sizes of the different continents in relation to the oceans.

It pleased Nathan to see a grad student acted as moderator. "Hello, my friends. It's time to get started if you'll please be seated." The attendees stopped their milling and found seats.

"I'm Alberto, and I like to start these meetings out with an appropriate joke. Who's got a good one this morning?"

A curly red-hair guy sitting next to Nathan stood up. "What happens when the chem-trails lift in Los Angeles?"

"What?" a girl wearing pink sunglasses asked.

"U.C.L.A."

"Oh, I get it. That's funny." She giggled. "You *see* Los Angeles. Cute. I'd like to know why chem-trails are even allowed?"

"We will be getting to that soon—so stay tuned." Alberto cleared his throat. "We have a guest speaker, but first, I want to welcome Nathan Benton, our new member. We're glad to have you, Bro."

Several warm welcomes were spoken and a couple of guys nearby, rose to slap his shoulders.

"Thanks. It's good to be here."

"The only two things I know for certain is that I'm going to die someday, and that the earth is flat."

"Amen!" a middle eastern man in the back called out. The twenty, or so, attending stood and clapped when the speaker entered the room. He raised a hand to silence them back into their seats.

"Let's all clap for this." He held up a worn Bible. "This is an old Wycliff. This one includes many books deleted after the original publishing; dates back in the fourteenth century.

"Many of these older banned books shed light on what we are coming to understand as our true dwelling place called earth. And several explain why the powers that be are afraid of those of us exposing the truth, such as the Book of Enoch."

The discussion proved lively, and Nathan enjoyed himself immensely.

"Hey, when did this become some kind of religious group?" One bushy haired guy interjected.

"We're open to seeking truth." The moderator answered

Before it all ended, on the monitor overhead, a large photo of a sun-god with its tongue sticking out appeared. Next to it was a photo of Albert Einstein with his tongue sticking out.

Written above the two photos, ***The lie is dictated by the global elite."***

"In closing, know the elite power brokers are heliocentric sun worshipers." The speaker shook his head then lifted the old Bible again. "This tells us they are fools. *'The wisdom of the world is foolish to those who are perishing.'* it says."

"And remember," he said it almost as an afterthought with the students leaving. "I'll pay a thousand dollars to anyone who can provide a real, untouched photo taken of the entire earth from outer space."

Nathan departed with a big smile on his face. On his way out, he studied a large poster of the NASA photos with the different drawn earths.

Above was a photo of a young NASA employee who created the earth rendering on his iPhone app. He titled it *"Of course, they are Photoshopped, but they HAVE to be!"*

Chapter Three

"And God said, 'Let there be a firmament in the midst of the waters, and let it divide the waters from the waters. And God made the firmament, and divided the waters which were under the firmament from the waters that were above the firmament: and it was so. And He called the firmament Heaven.'"
Genesis 1: 6-8

Back in Virginia, Sue wandered around the house, ending up as she often did in Nathan's room, forlorn and restless. Her husband poked his head in the room. "Come on, darling. Let's get out of the house to the Farmers Market."

"Great! This empty nest brings me down sometimes. It was bad enough when Gwen left, jetting around the world. I know being a big-time reporter was her dream, but . . . And now, Nathan all the way in California for college?"

Life had been an adjustment since both retired. Attending a home church group was their favorite activity. Her linguist husband enjoyed studying the Bible in Latin, Greek, and Hebrew. It was a far cry from Washington D.C. and training diplomats for their assignments.

She missed her art classes, teaching painting to young and old alike. Her years of teaching, in some ways, were more relaxing than working their small ranch in the Virginia foothills, purchased specifically for the golden years.

During the height of Covid, she and Russ avoided all of the mandates and protocols, opting to buy an RV and head South that winter instead. Respite came when they settled for the season on South Padre Island off the Texas coast.

How quickly they made so many fast friends surprised them both. Most were faithful folks, warning against a deep-state government, the United Nations, the WHO, and the World Economic Forum that were all implementing evil worldwide plans.

With such horrific news, they banded together in an RV Camp study group to search their Bibles for the truth behind all the worldly agendas such as plan-demics, global warming, modifications of food, and depopulation.

At the end of that winter season, the group came to the conclusion to trust in the Lord for health, provision and protection. They all agreed to keep sharing the Good News of Jesus and live each day anticipating His imminent return.

Home on the ranch, Russ was tired of chores. Nearby, Sue crouched over her flower beds, planting marigolds along the long driveway. She loved her wide-brimmed pink hat, his thirtieth wedding anniversary present he gave her earlier that month.

Cupping his hands, Russ called out. "Hey! Maybe we need to take a road trip west in the RV."

He looked longingly at the small Thor hybrid. "Don't you miss traveling? I love taking off in our home on wheels. It's so good on gas—"

"What?" Sue cajoled him. "That might be a good idea, but Nathan has barely been in college a month. Do you think it's a good idea? We don't want to be hovering parents, do we?"

"I see no harm. Visit some friends along the way."

She stood, stretched her back, then started up the drive toward him. "I know what you're thinking darlin'. . ."

"We could swing by the Myrtle Beach Mission Conference on the way. Take a month or so. We can't forget the Gospel commission you know."

She turned her palms skyward making that face he loved before finally breaking a smile. "You're funny Russ Benton."

The following week on the long Myrtle Beach Strand, Russ and his wife ran into a group of people clamoring about a big man in a yellow hardhat. Upon investigating, he found himself in the middle of a documentary film.

"It's called *Flat-out Truth – Flat-out Lies! And we get paid!*" The young boy seemed so excited. "I'm helping with the equipment on set, too, and I just became a teenager this year!" The nametag on his lanyard read David.

Sue leaned in and whispered, "He's quite tall for thirteen, don't you think?"

"See the man in the yellow hat? He's a retired USDS Master Surveyor, and he's willing to pay one hundred thousand dollars to anybody who can prove there's any curvature at all on Mrytle Beach. From South Carolina, it goes all the way down towards Georgia, you know."

"That's a lot of money to gamble on it being level, David." Russ grimaced. "Seems your boss must be quite confident."

"He is!" The young teen's eyes widened. "It's a long stretch of sixty miles of continuous beach! Longest in the country! And so far, no one has taken him up on the offer. He surveyed the whole thing and guess what?"

"What?" Russ and Sue answered in unison.

"It's flat as a pancake. All sixty miles worth. Know what that means?" The exuberant youth answered his own question. "It's flaaaa…"

"It's flat." Russ ended the young man's sentence. "It means the earth is not a globe."

Sue leaned back on her husband, asking rhetorically, "We keep running into this one, don't we, sweetie?"

"Well, I gotta go." Young David turned and ran toward the surveyor who signaled for him to come.

Quickly spinning around, running backwards, he asked a final question. "You know what else says it isn't a globe?" The boy evidently loved answering his own questions. "The Bible! It says it over and over again! Just look and see for yourselves."

In record time, Russ drove the RV across the states then headed south along Highway 1 on California's Pacific Coast. The following morning, he had arranged a surprise meeting with their two children.

Sue, always so meticulous with organization, pulled a map and folder from an overhead compartment. "Our best bet is to camp overnight in Carpinteria, near Santa Barbara. There's an RV Park overlooking the ocean with one spot left open. Shall I book it?"

"I'm always amazed how you navigate without using any technology." Russ smiled. "Glad we're traveling old school."

Suddenly, they noticed a line of cars pulled to the side of the highway. Drivers milled around speaking with each other outside of their vehicles. Doors remained flung wide.

Shading their eyes, the people stared at the sky.

What was happening?

Russ veered around one truck blocking the road then pulled the compact RV over. "I'm going to check out the commotion. You stay in the car until I see what's going on."

Like the others, he exited the RV and peered up. A loud noise sounded. The sky appeared to crack wide open. A fire lit up the coastal skyline in a red hue. A surfer-type in a tank top answered Russ' unasked question.

"It's Space X! You know, one of Elon Musk's rockets!"

"Why is it veering sideways?" Russ noticed the ascent seemed like such an odd angle. "Why doesn't it just head straight up into space?"

"Don't ask me any tough stuff, man. Something to do with physics, or curvature, or . . . you know . . ."

A moment later, Russ leaned against the side of the RV with his wife, watching mesmerized as the Space X rocket angled sideways, almost disappearing. Then suddenly, a bright flash lit up the sky.

Had the nose of the rocket hit the dome firmament?

A slice of heaven appeared to open wide, shining with a hazy blue light. The disintegrating rocket seemed to fall in pieces leaving an expanding glow. The sky seemingly cracked wide open.

The crack left something like rippling waves cascading over many waters. In the same manner as a boat wake fans out, the glow spread ever outward as one lone rocket engine thrust onward. It looked a lot like an insect trying to fly in a stream.

"Has to be a decent enough rocket, assuming that was the main core. It just keeps pushing and pushing. Check to see how long it lasts."

His wife scanned her watch.

The sky opening was wide aglow in a hazy light. It seemed the rocket kept pushing and pushing."

"It's been over four minutes, Russ. What do you make of this?"

"It appears that it's reaching the deeper waters. The waves seem to be dissipating the same as if it were descending into the dense water found on the bottom of the sea."

"That reminds me of how in Genesis it says that God divided the waters under the firmament, from the waters above the firmament."

The people standing outside their cars and trucks were lining alongside Highway 1. Perplexed and unaware of what they witnessed. Did they think it was simply fuselage being jettisoned from a semi-successful launch?

The surfer fellow leaned against his short surfboard, propped up by a roadway sign.

"Elon Musk is the man! He has apparatus that automatically locates these incredible flying machines in the ocean after splashdown. then reuses them over and over."

"How could he know that?"

"He doesn't, my darling."

Finally back on the two-lane highway, Sue remained silent. Russ was deep in thought as well, contemplating what he had witnessed. Nathan had been a big proponent of a level earth.

Maybe his son wasn't as far off center as he thought. Russ assumed it was a phase his son was going through. Still, could there really be anything to it? He couldn't wrap his head around it.

How would his son know such a thing? Nathan had tried to convince them more times than he could count, but he was just an impressionable kid.

Someone like Elon Musk though . . . He must know things a regular person had no access to.

Could the billionaire actually know about a flat earth under a dome?

Russ recalled a documentary video their son had sent describing the firmament from the book of Genesis. How the windows of heaven opened to rain Noah's flood upon the earth.

According to the documentary, both the U.S. Military and the Soviets had tried to blow a hole in the dome over the earth using nuclear bombs in 1962. The U.S. secretly referred to theirs as "Operation Fishbowl."

The Soviets had conducted five known high-altitude nuclear blasts in an effort to break through the dome during the early sixties. Eventually, a pact was signed between the countries after they mutually concluded it was impenetrable.

The so-called tests had caused a wake of radiation to rain down over land and seas though. People, too.

"Well, I guess we'll have plenty to share with our son tomorrow." Sue glanced his way. "Do you think he was right, Russ? Could he have been telling us the truth?"

"I don't see how we could deny it now. And Gwen, too. She may not be so far off . . . "

Sue yawned. "We're supposed to meet her at the hotel tomorrow around five. It sure is going to be nice to have a steaming hot shower that isn't so confining." She made her way toward the back and the RV's cramped bathroom.

"Agreed. I'm ready to be done driving for this day." Within minutes, he turned into the oceanside RV park his wife booked for the night.

Prior to turning off the solar lantern at bedtime, Sue took his hand. "Let's say we are on a Flat Earth and not spinning in space. Why would it be so important? It isn't a salvation issue, right?"

"Well, for a start, it says that all liars will not inherit the Kingdom of Heaven. So, if you believe what the Bible says about it and then you deny it . . ."

Chiming in, Sue interrupted. "Or if you're a part of NASA, or even someone like Elon Musk, who knows the truth but don't come clean . . . Their gooses will be cooked in the end, won't they?"

"I love your grandma's sayings. Cooked gooses indeed." Russ laughed and leaned over for a goodnight kiss.

As they drifted to sleep, Sue whispered a sweet prayer; "Thank you for showing us Your glory, Lord."

A gentle ocean breeze answered, rocking the RV.

Chapter Four

"Keep that which is committed to thy trust, avoiding profane and vain babblings, and oppositions from science, falsely so called." 1 Timothy 6:20

Nathan arrived early to the palatial hotel, marveling at its opulence. He took the elevator to the fourteenth floor, found her room, and knocked.

The minute she opened the door, he was surprised how he missed his big Sis.

"Nathan!" She threw her arms around him. "It's so good to see you! Come in, come in."

Wow, he had missed her.

"Nathan!" She threw her arms around him . . ."It's so good to see you! Come in, come in."

"I know, me, too. Aww Sis, I'm so glad Mom and Pop planned this trip and got us together. What time are they due?"

"Not for another hour. Want some kombucha?"

"Got milk?"

"Sorry, no."

"Water will do. I'm glad to have some time to talk before they get here. They think I'm a lunatic, you know."

"Oh, they do not. What's been going on in your neck of the woods?"

"Well, I have a Level Earth group, like minds and all that. Meets on Tuesday nights, but all the guys are still blinded."

"Why's that?" She handed him a water bottle.

"Well, most of them do believe in the scientific truth that we're not on a round globe ball, but I'm the only one there who believes the Biblical truth of it. I don't think any of them know God."

"Humph. Isn't it crazy? I mean what they believe in takes even more faith."

"As a whole, it's a Godless campus. They all believe in evolution, aliens, and even magic. One of them has been trying to convince me the world was seeded by extraterrestrials."

"Oh, shut the door." His sister shook her head. "How can people be so blind when God's glorious creation is so obvious?"

"Let me show you something." Nathan swiped his cellphone and opened his BibleGateway app then tapped up a Scripture. *"And for this cause God shall send them a strong delusion, that they should believe a lie, that they all might be damned who believed not the truth but have pleasure in unrighteousness."*

"Oh, wow. So, because they don't love the truth, God hands them over to a strong delusion? That's why they believe such ridiculous stuff?"

"It's the Word."

"So all those who are behind the spinning globe ball are lying and will be damned? Sounds a little harsh."

"I wouldn't want to be in their shoes. No way, no how. You know it says in Revelation that all liars will burn in the lake of fire. Maybe it's for those intentionally lying about it."

"Or maybe it's for those who know the truth deep down but choose to believe the lies of science over the truth of God."

"Wow, when you put it that way—but I'm just still not that sure about the earth being flat, Brother. I don't judge you. To each his own." Her voice trailed off then she giggled. "A fake moon landing is one thing, but a Flat Earth?"

She went back and forth with him until he lost track of the time. When he checked his phone, he jumped up.

"We better get down to the lobby, Sis. They may be here already."

When the elevator doors opened, he spotted his parents waiting on a couch by a huge palm. His mother stood. "Nathan! Gwen! You two sure are a sight for sore eyes."

Hugs were plentiful until his dad took charge. "Anybody hungry?"

"Yes, sir, I sure am."

Gwen smiled. "I made us reservations in the dining room."

"Does your station pay for all this?" Mother Sue was curious.

"Certainly! I couldn't afford it!" They all laughed.

Over dinner his parents described the incredible SpaceX flight they witnessed the night before. "It hit something. . ."

"I've heard about that!" Nathan sat forward. "I'm glad to hear you're taking the Flat Earth concept seriously. That's awesome. A few truthers already released some amazing videos on that launch up off the Pacific Coast Highway."

"What's a *Truther?*" Pop looked skeptical.

"A person who will stop at nothing to expose the truth. They're like a dog digging for a bone and won't be satisfied until they get to the whole truth of a matter."

"Well, that's our Gwendolyn to be sure. I was so proud of you for exposing the president's affair. I only wish you could have tied him to Chef Tafari's death."

"Still working on that one, Mom…"

After comparing stories about their recent goings-on—everyone but Gwen—they were amazed to find their Level Earth conversations had led to questions about salvation.

"Well, I guess you can say we are of one accord on this." Russ lifted up both hands towards them all. "It's brought our family together, having the same concerns."

His mother turned to Gwen. "What is really tugging at me was reading over 200 Bible verses, that Nathan sent us. They clearly describe God's stationary creation. When we are wrestling with these things, the scripture helps uncover the truth. I know that, you are a big Truther." She laughed and leaned into her daughter.

"I love you, Mom."

Over dessert, Gwen lowered her voice and shared her assignment. "I interviewed someone who gave me a video. It's a copy of the original films showing the moon landings were all done in a movie studio." A hush fell over the table.

"But don't tell anyone!"

"Of course not. But doesn't that put you in danger? Are you sure no one on the wrong side knows about your interview, honey?"

"Don't worry, Sue. She's in God's hands" Russ glanced at his daughter. "I'm not surprised though."

"I knew it!" Nathan slapped the table. "So proud of you, Sis! No wonder you mentioned a fake moon landing. . ."

"Well, at this point, you can't tell anyone. I'm still putting the story together and have no idea how the network's going to respond. They squelched my report on the Climate Summit. No telling what they'll do with this."

"Well, it is earth-shattering news. Talk about one of the world's biggest lies." His mother just shook her head. "Dad and I are proud of you two. You both really want to make a difference in the world…but of course I'm not biased at all!"

After dinner, they took a long walk around the lush grounds of the Hillside Hotel. The stars were out in full force—not the Hollyweird kind. Rare in the L.A. area for such clear skies, but the Santa Ana winds had picked up and cleared the air.

His father sauntered along, bringing up the rear, visiting with his daughter. With her previous boyfriend issues, he encouraged her to wait for the right guy. "Grandma always advised us to find someone with the same values. Someone of the faith."

"I really miss her."

"She was a gem of a mom, too." He gazed up at the night sky hopefully. "I know she's happy with the Lord though."

"It must have been hard for her with Grandpa Benton. Has he ever believed in anything other than working so hard?"

"Dad is a romantic at heart, Gwen. Always had a hard time showing it, but everyone knew Grandma was his one true love. Remember she asked us to keep praying for him to find Jesus."

"Oh, I will. Thanks, Dad. I admit I've been feeling a little lost with work these days myself…"

"You know your mom and I pray for both of you daily."

Nathan slowed his mom a bit and let the two dragging behind catch up. It was so great having his parents getting on board with what he knew for so long to be true. He wanted nothing more than to be on the same page about the shape of the earth.

Now to get his stubborn sister to believe.

Palms swayed in the strong winds. "Hey, did I tell you I'm saving for a professional telescope?"

"Tonight would be a great one to study the skies, wouldn't it?" His sister gazed upwards. "What are you wanting to see? Anything in particular?"

"Just want to check on some ideas."

"I thought I heard you two talking about Grandpa Benton." Mom slipped her arm into and around Pop's. Nathan had always appreciated them showing their affection for one another.

"Did you hear he finally quit working on Wall Street?"

"What?"

"What?" His sister had his same reaction, almost simultaneously. It sure didn't sound like the grandpa he knew.

"He retired?"

"He'd never retire." Gwen slapped his arm in play. "What'd he quit for? He's been married to his job forever! What's he doing?"

"He bought a sailboat." His father stated it so matter-of-factly. "Says he's sailing around the world."

"That sounds so unlike Grandpa!"

Gwen loved the New York skyline. Flying into LaGuardia gave her a sense of home every time. She grabbed a taxi and went straight to the Network where she handed over her treasures. The Kubrick tapes.

After a quick scan, Boss Roger became irate.

What was the matter with him?

"I'm not mad at you." He slammed her folder onto his desk. "Who is ever going to believe this? A fake moon landing covered up for over fifty years?"

"You're the one who gave me the assignment, Roger. It's the truth!"

Rubbing his belly, he paused, and she could see his wheels turning. "It may be good for the ratings, though. I wonder . . ."

Using both hands on the chair's arms, her boss pushed his considerable weight up and stood upright, still leaning on his desk.

"Listen, I like all the background footage exposing the NASA fraud you put together, but you need an eyewitness, someone willing to go on the record."

Reaching in her studio case, Gwen retrieved the video recorder given to her at the end of her interview in the bungalow. She set it on a corner of the desk.

"Turn off your cell phone, Roger."

"Why?"

"Your computer, too. Turn it off, all the way off. Is there a router in here?"

"No. Why do you want me to turn—"

"Just do it. Humor me."

He obliged her, and she hit the play button.

Hearing and seeing Kubrick on the screen, her boss slumped back into his seat with his eyes riveted. The closeup of the famous director came into focus.

"That's Stanley Kubrick."

"Yes, sir. Just watch this interview."

In the video playback, an off-screen male asked a question. "Why me? Why not CNN?"

"Don't trust them." Kubrick responds.

"Is this about an upcoming film?"

"No—not about a new movie—about one I made in the past. A confession."

"What did you do? Cheat on your wife? Plagiarize?"

"I'd never do that. Do you want to hear me out or not? I can always find someone else."

"No, that won't be necessary. I'm ready to listen to whatever it is you have to say."

"This is about a movie I made that no one knows about, even though millions have seen it."

"Intriguing."

"I perpetrated a fraud involving the United States Government and NASA. I'm sure you've heard the rumors."

"The . . . moon landing?"

"That's right, but there was no landing. The whole thing was faked. The moon landings were all bogus. I know because I filmed them."

"You're serious, here?"

"As a heart-attack." Kubrick stared into the camera. "Dead serious. The conspiracy theorists got it right on this one. I don't know about Kennedy's death but this one is true."

"Why? Why would you do it? Why are you telling me all this now?"

"Don't you think it's important for people to know the truth?"

"Certainly."

"Well, people the world over deceived by a massive con! An unparalleled sham committed against them. They should know the truth! Their suspicions of their government should be confirmed, justified. Don't you think?"

"If you don't mind me saying, sir, you look a little haggard."

"Too much bourbon. Too much pressure, stress, guilt. Conflict every minute of every day."

"Do you feel bad about it?"

Kubrick looked away distracted then back. "I do, but I also feel a bit . . . proud of it as well. Like I said, constant divergence."

"What are you proud of, if I may ask."

The man closed his eyes and shook his head like he was speaking with an idiot. "You're here to ask, aren't you? I'm proud of pulling it off. Humph, it's the greatest hoax of all time. My masterpiece."

"But you can't take credit for it or talk about it."

"What do you think I'm doing right now, young man?"

"With all due respect, sir. I believe you're signing your own death warrant."

"And that's where the kicker comes in."

"No one is to know until after my death."

"Right. You're telling me to wait? What ten to fifteen years after your death? So then, is this signing my own death warrant?"

"You're the one who wanted the scoop."

The video went black. That old proverbial dropped pin? Well, a deaf man could have heard it. Roger didn't move. The still silence reigned for over a minute.

"Oh, my."

The large man was first to utter a sound or move a muscle—a comb motion over his hairless scalp. "What is it with you Gwen Benton Sharpe? This is the kind of thing people lose their lives over."

"Or jobs?"

"Lot of good a job will do either one of us if this gets out. We'll be toast."

Roger finally spread a smile, then back in character with a stern face, he gave her a wink. "Let's not tell anyone about this. Not just yet."

"But—"

"Not yet. Let's let it soak it in. Remember what Kubrick himself said. 'I'm *dead* serious.' Then he died shortly thereafter."

"His final film exposed the Illuminati and Masonic elite, *Eyes Wide Shut*, filmed at a Rothchild mansion in Great Britain." Gwen referred to her notes.

"Listen. We've got a dragon by the tail with this one." Deep wrinkles in Roger's forehead seemed accentuated. "Keep researching. Under the radar, of course, but don't make a move—you hear me?—not a move without talking to me first."

"Roger that!" Her hand went to her mouth, covering a grin. "Ooops. Sorry about that."

Not even a hint of a smile on his face, he waved a finger, motioning her out of his office. "I'll keep the video locked up in here. . .let it go this time."

Chapter Five

"He shall have dominion also from sea to sea, and from the rivers unto the ends of the earth."   Psalm 72:8

Sam Benton was on Wall Street trading commodities for nearly two decades. After the death of his wife of forty years, he considered giving up his life of a gambler—using other people's money.

When the crash came, he set his guardian decision to cash in his chips. What he'd stashed away in his portfolio paid off his home, his debts, and bought him a nice used sailboat.

Not just any old sailboat though, the *Juggernaut,* a fifty-foot Westsail, a prize on any budget. He'd longed for a craft in stellar condition, one that included every amenity and electronic device known to man.

A boat that would allow him to accomplish a lifetime dream . . . circumnavigate the earth.

He intended to set out alone on his altruistic quest and sail around the world in less than a year—an adequate amount of time for some exploration along the way. His timing seemed to work well with the family, too.

Busy with lives of their own, his son, Russ and wife Sue were always so involved with their Christian causes. Most of their time now was spent on their small ranch, in the mission fields, or conferences.

They were all about sharing the faith. He'd kept up with their travels through Gwennie. She often invited him to dinner since she got the television job. His granddaughter also kept him abreast of her brother off to U.C.L.A.

He'd thought about inviting Nathan to go with him, but the boy needed an education.

Sam kept himself fit with regular workouts, while steering clear of doctors and hospitals over the years. He hated their pills and their vaccines. On that one point, he agreed with his son.

Injections were not to be trusted. He was thankful the grandkids were also resigned to stay shot free.

Russ hadn't put up much of a fuss when he told him about leaving on the voyage. He thought back to their conversation.

"Not to worry, Son. Since losing your mom, I've been lost. A sail around the world is just what I need."

If only she were still alive and could accompany him.

Within weeks of his announcement, the entire family came dockside to christen the vessel and bid him *Bon Voyage*. Well, all but his mother, ninety-seven and living with a younger cousin out west.

They presented him a grocery cart of provisions and one very special present. Opening the white gift box, Sam reached inside and brought out a captain's hat—the perfect gift.

"We hereby increase your Naval rank from Ensign to Captain, Grandpa!"

"Well thank you, Nathan."

Though there had been a certain amount of father and son contention over the years, Russ blessed him with a round of hearty cheers.

Before casting off, Nathan came up from below deck. The boy seemed reluctant to leave the ship.

"Want to come along there, Grandson?"

"That would be incredible, but . . . I've got school. Someday, Grandpa . . ."

Below deck, Nathan left his grandfather a letter. It would be five long months at sea before the old man found and read the letter. It changed forever how he viewed the world, and it would change his heart.

Time alone at sea gave Sam many hours of reflection. As a young man when his son Russell was still in preschool, Sam enlisted with the Naval reserves to be a chaplain.

While away on a summer deployment at a remote base in Alaska, he had sent for his wife and one-year-old daughter to join him for a couple of weeks. Little Russell stayed with his grandmother.

He remembered standing on the small landing strip, waiting with such anticipation. As if in slow motion, he watched in horror as the military air transport carrying his wife and daughter crashed.

The pilot lost control on a long stretch of flat ice. The plane flipped upside down. All inside perished except for two people—the pilot and Sam's wife. Eleven souls met their maker that day, including their precious daughter.

His wife, Sandra, suffered a broken back and never fully recovered—or would carry more children.

Later, he had discovered mysterious circumstances shrouded the pilot error. The man, a young cousin of the commander, went undisciplined, and the whole matter was covered up.

Those were the worst days of his life.

His faith waned. Unforgiveness had always lingered in the back of his mind, toward the pilot—and toward God. Sam had counseled the young man several times over a drinking problem.

The young man mocked anything to do with God.

Sam also carried the guilt of being emotionally unavailable to his wife and son afterwards, blaming himself for pressing his wife to come to Alaska in the first place.

There was one bright light in it all. Fondly, he recalled the day they adopted a precious infant daughter they named Janice.

After his enlistment ended, he'd switched his focus and pursued the excitement of high finance. He tackled his work on Wall Street with a fervor, ending up in International Arbitrage.

Yet, deep inside, he felt lost in the world. He lost many years in a dark monetary milieu that never delivered on the promise of riches and fulfillment.

Sandra remained stellar though, immersing herself in helping others, studying scripture, and sharing her faith. Always, she prayed for him to return to his true love, Jesus.

He had no need for faith anymore though.

The day after his parents visit in his humanities class, a girl sitting near Nathan brought up an interesting topic. "With all the transhumans they're talking about, will it be the ending of humans? The end of the world?"

The professor laughed. "What exactly are you referring to when you say transhumans?"

Nathan admired how the pretty Asian girl responded in such a secular campus environment.

"You know—science is mixing human and animal DNA. With gene editing and technology, they try to improve on people. What God made. Even putting computer chips in people's brains!"

She went on to boldly share her faith about reading the Book of Revelation, *The Apocalypse,* she was certain the end times were upon the earth.

The humanities professor stopped her in mid-sentence. "Maybe these are topics for your science or theology professors."

Nathan took notice of his classmates' cross necklace, then hurried to catch up and speak with her after class ended. "So, you are a Christian then?" He nodded at her cross.

"Yes, I am." She smiled. "My name is Myiah. We flee from Myanmar, Burma, after much persecution. Many die— my grandparents and a cousin were killed."

"Oh wow. I'm sorry to hear that. My name is Nathan."

"We barely escape. They burned our home." She bowed her head. "We left with Jesus though."

He answered with something about God being sovereign on the throne then changed the subject.

"I love it that you think these are the last days. The Word says no one knows the day or hour but the Father alone, right?"

"Yes, but does that mean, you think, we can know the week or the month?"

"Hmm, never thought of it like that. Maybe we can study some Scripture together later on."

"I like that." Myiah blushed.

Before leaving, he acquired her contact information and promised to call her.

That weekend, Nathan's turn to share at his Level Earth group came up. He had been reluctant, knowing the scientific and nerdy-minded young men in attendance would mock him for interjecting his faith.

Myiah's boldness gave him courage though.

If just one person responded . . .

"Listen. You guy know I believe in a Level Earth as much as anyone here. The difference is that my understanding doesn't come only from science but from the Creator."

Murmurs sounded across the room, and Nathan held up a hand to silence the skeptics.

"Wait, just wait and hear what I have to say. First off, who can tell me the name of the first man into space—you know, the first guy to reach the stratosphere?"

"August Piccard!" Someone shouted out from the group.

"Right! Piccard was a friend of Albert Einstein. He rode in a metal pod attached to a tall and thin hot air balloon. It was launched in France in 1939, on a still cloudless day. He shot straight up miles into the deep blue sky, high enough to observe the earth was not a globe.

Piccard reported that he observed a flat disk with upturned edges."

Good. They were listening.

"Piccard questioned that if he hovered the balloon in one place, on a still day without much wind, why did the earth not rotate beneath him? After two hours with a globe spinning at a thousand miles per hour, he would no longer be airborne over France. He should have ended up somewhere east of Florence, Italy. But Piccard landed near where he had launched in France."

Nathan used a laser pointer highlighting a video re-creation on the screens.

"Why do you suppose that is? Scoffers ask, 'What does it matter?' Really, why is Level Earth important to you? More importantly, in my humble opinion, is why is it so important to the one true God who I know in my heart created us?" Reaching down, he projected ten points onto the two large screens they used in the meeting room.

Earth Lies:
1. There is no God or Creator.
2. The Bible is a false narrative written by men.
3. Religion cripples Mankind.
4. Science will save Mankind.
5. Aliens seeded the planet and are real.
6. The occult, sorcery, magic, horoscopes and earth mysteries are the answers.
7. Life is an illusionary construct.
8. Heliocentric theory and gravity are real.
9. Fallen angels are gods and created us.
10. Space programs and astronauts are real.

Earth Truth:
1. God is real and created all.
2. Level Earth is real.
3. The Anti-Christ will promote the alien delusion.
4. He will claim to bring peace & safety with prosperity and be the savior of 'Planet Earth.'
5. Sudden destruction will come.
6. Jesus will return and rescue those who believe in Him.

Several in his audience looked perplexed. They seemed interested, but Nathan figured many had never been exposed to the true God of the Bible.

He explained the very first verse in the Bible, *"In the beginning God created the heaven and the earth"* reveals the creation wasn't from an accidental cosmic explosion.

"God made all things, and all creation is sacred, special to Him. You are special to Him. The earth is special to Him. He created it level—flat, stationary, and told us exactly that in the Bible says. It is exactly how God created it to be, with a firmament dome cover.

"Many of you believe this, but you still believe in Harry Potter, aliens, and traveling out in space, too. Truth and lies don't go together."

"Why not?" A student from India spoke out abruptly.

"Take aliens for example. There's a delusion going on right now. In Revelation 13:13, Scripture says the Anti-Christ will come and deceive many, even calling down fire from above. Aliens are really demons."

After the healthy discussion, he ended his talk and passed out pamphlets clarifying each point. Outside in the campus courtyard, one of the attendees approached.

"Hey, Nathan. I liked your talk." He stuck out his hand. "I'm Jake. You got a minute?"

"Sure. Good to meet you, Jake."

"It's about all the Bible stuff. Do you really believe all that?"

"I do. It was a catalyst to my belief in and understanding of a Level Earth model."

"Really? Hmmm. I might be interested in hearing a little more about all that. You know, if you have any more information. Maybe we could get together sometime, but . . . keep it private?"

"Ah, so not let your friends guess you've gone off the deep end, seeing you with me?"

"No-no, it isn't like that. You're a good guy. Pretty smart, too."

"Thanks." The older student stood towering over him. "What are you anyway? Six feet five?"

"Six-six."

"You're on the football team, right?"

"Yeah, a quarterback that sees no action."

"Why's that?

"I'm backup. Been sitting the bench since my freshman year. I'm a senior now. Not much chance I'll get a shot at making it to the bigtime."

"You want to play professionally? The NFL?"

"Who doesn't? It isn't going to happen though. I'll teach or something, but I'm failing math."

There had to be a reason the guy reached out to him. "Maybe I can help with that. We can talk about the Bible."

"Sure."

"Great. We can meet in the library."

A couple of other students walked past, turned, and called out. "Hey." "It's Big Jake!" He was obviously well known.

"You know Jake, God has a plan for your life. We can set a day and place to get together, and I can text you a couple of videos if you want—and some writings, too."

"Uh, should I have one of those books? Do you have extras?"

"You mean the Bible?"

"Yeah—doubt if the bookstore has any."

"Sure," Nathan gave a broad smile. "I'll bring an extra one when we get together."

At the Network in Manhattan, her boss called Gwen back into his office just before she left for the day.

"Listen, tomorrow there's a big press conference. It's been sixty years since they held the ticker tape parade for the first astronauts on the moon."

"Must be sponsored by Freemasons."

Roger rolled his eyes, chiding her. "Buzz Aldren is the only one left, but he will be there. I want you to go rattle Buzz Lightyear's cage for us."

Man, he was really getting into the spirit of it "On it, Boss. They'll never know what space debris hit him."

"Remember. Not a word on the Kubrick thing."

"No, sir. My lips are sealed."

Researching into the night Gwen discovered moon rocks sold by NASA were proven to be petrified wood, confirmed by several independent laboratories.

She located another video of an obviously inebriated Buzz Aldrin at a book signing and he ended up punching some guy.

A young man holding up a Bible made a simple request: "Sir, will you swear with your hand on this Bible, by Holy God, that you really walked on the moon?"

Aldrin stood and smacked the poor kid in the face!

The next morning, it surprised Gwen to see such few members of the press in attendance. The historic moon landing event had been so highly touted earlier.

Hosted at Rockefeller Plaza in a large banquet room, the first NASA astronaut to stand behind the podium seemed dumbfounded when a little girl posed a simple question.

"How is it possible that a helicopter or balloon floating in the same location for hours on end, stays in one spot?"

The answer seemed obvious, even to a seven-year-old.

Finally, Aldrin took to the stage to rescue the younger astronaut, but the little girl hit Buzz even harder with another question.

"Why hasn't anybody been back to the moon in such a long time?"

What a precocious child. Gwen had prepared this same question. It had been over fifty years since the moon landing aired on TV. The little girl had scooped her.

The answer from Buzz bordered on the psychotic, his dark eyes rolling in a controlled manner. "That isn't a question from a little girl."

An awkward pause ensued.

Gwen stood. "Well, she didn't get it from me, but it was one of my questions, too." She motioned to the room. "I think we all want to know the answer, Astronaut Aldrin."

Buzz squirmed in a patronizing soft-pitched voice. "I want to know…because I think I know…because we didn't go there…and that's the way it happened. And if it didn't happen, then it's nice to know why…"

A stunned silence settled over the room. What had he said. Gwen repeated it verbatim in her head. Had he just admitted they hadn't gone to the moon? At all?

Because we didn't go there… That's what he had said.

In a flash of cameras, a handler raced Buzz offstage before another word broke the eerie silence.

Back at the office, her news director read over her story and checked out her cameraman's footage. Buzz revealing to a seven-year-old and his network's reporter that he never stepped foot on the moon.

No one had.

A while later, it seemed the whole office erupted. Roger yelled at someone over the phone. His booming voice echoed loud and clear through the entire newsroom.

He's going to bat for the story!

Gwen was elated.

"This is real news!" Roger ranted on to his higher-up. "A fake moon landing! We've got the film director and now one of the astronauts who supposedly went admitting he never did. It's all on camera!"

The tug of war with words ended with slamming his phone down.

Her elation faded as her emotions came back to earth. Mainstream media would never allow any of her film or report to be aired. All her work was in vain.

That night, after becoming even more intrigued with the deception, she called her Flat Earther brother.

"Did you see the news reel I sent you at my press conference today with Buzz Aldrin?"

"I can't believe he spilled the beans to a little girl and to my sister!"

"They're not going to let us run the story."

"Don't be surprised how high the cover-up goes, Sis." Nathan's Level Earth group had prepared her with this insight.

"Oh, I wouldn't, Little Brother."

Over the years, his sister had been a Flat Earth doubter, so he figured he might as well seize the opportunity. "So, does this mean you'll be changing your mind on the earth shape then?"

"Well, I'm guess I'm maybe starting to believe. I mean if we never went to the moon, then we've probably have never been in space, and I guess those pictures of the planet from space could have been faked . . . I mean if the moon landing was."

"It isn't a planet, Sis. It's a level plane with a firmament above exactly like the Bible says. The sun, moon, and stars are close, not far off, and they are lights in the firmament."

"Oh, Nate-the-Great. You're so sure, aren't you?"

"Of course, I am. Did you know the moon is translucent? It's possible to see right through it at times—most likely a cooler plasma type of light. How can you land on a translucent object and pick up rocks to bring back?"

"Petrified wood."

"What?"

"I discovered last night the moon rocks NASA sold are nothing more than petrified wood. So the moon is a light?"

"Yes, it is, and like I've said all along, we're not spinning about endlessly in space."

The phone went silent. He waited for her to respond, ready to debate. Was that breathing? Had the connection dropped? Or was she just processing the information?

"Gwen? You still there?"

"Yeah."

"Could it be, dear sister, that God put you here for such a time as this, like Queen Esther? I mean, look at the stories He's given you. Please tell me you don't think it's a coincidence."

"Oh, so I'm like Queen Esther in the Bible? You're so funny." Gwen laughed. "I don't know, Nate. I don't think it's coincidental. How could it be? Queen Esther, huh? I always loved that story."

*"And God made the firmament, and divided the waters which were under the firmament, from the waters which were above the firmament, **and it was so...**"* Genesis 1:7

Chapter Six

"And they that be wise shall shine as the brightness of the firmament; and they that turn many to righteousness as the stars forever and ever."　　　　　　　　Daniel 12:3

Back on campus, Professor Thompsen left a message on Nathan's cell phone.

"Listen, you may be onto something with this Biblical shape of the Earth. Being the doubting Thomas type, I've done some calculations. Hoping you come to this week's symposium."

That weekend, it thrilled Nathan that the professor presented a geo stationary earth model. On the monitor, he'd created several mathematical formulas.

"This spinning world most believe in supposedly travels around the solar system at a speed of sixty-six thousand six hundred miles per hour. They say the curve is point six hundred sixty-six feet to the mile squared. Interesting figures they come up with, don't you think?"

Six-six-six, twice. The number of Lucifer.

Professor Thompsen leaned over to pick up a stack of papers then continued. "The curvature of the earth drop formula they use is eight inches times a mile squared. But anyone who travels to a tall mountain will see the horizon stays level far beyond the supposed limit.

"How are we able to view the Chicago skyline from across Lake Michigan in Canada over fifty miles away? It would be impossible on a curved Earth.

"According to the globe model—which I point out is just a model—the Earth pulls things down and causes them to accelerate at 9.8m/s².

"They say the Earth also rotates. But we know that rotating objects push things outwards due to centrifugal force. For example, if you were to take a basketball, put water on it, and then spin it, the water flies out away from the ball.

"This is the same force you feel when a car moves in a circle. You're slung to the outside. So, if the Earth is spinning, it should exert a force that causes things to accelerate outwards.

"Here's a question. Do you feel the Earth spinning right now? Unless you've spun yourself around, you don't. Since we don't feel the earth rotating, doesn't observation tell us we are not?

"A common counterargument is you can only feel motion if you accelerate, but that neglects that a rotation is an acceleration—an inwards acceleration. So clearly, something isn't adding up.

"Not only can you do the math to prove that under the spinning model, objects cannot fall at 9.8m/s²."

The Professor pulled out an old-style, large white board from the side of the platform and began to accelerate his talk while quickly writing figures out with a blue marker.

"So to calculate the centrifugal force, we use this equation, $F = mv^2/r$. The force of gravity is $F=mg$. So, the net force would be $F = mg - mv^2/r = m(g - v^2)/r$. To calculate the centrifugal acceleration, we use a $= v^2/r =$ (460m/s ^{2})/(6,371,000m) = 0.033m/s² "

Nathan had empathy for all those not to speedy in math. Though it was all a little over his head, he was able to keep up and was fascinated by Doctor Thompsen's calculations.

Big Jake, on the other hand, sat across the room studying something on the wall, obviously lost.

"This means that the outward centrifugal acceleration of objects is 0.033m/s². The downward acceleration of objects due to gravity alone is 9.8m/s², meaning the total acceleration of an object is 9.8m/s² minus 0.033m/s² = 9.767 m/s².

"We have determined objects fall at 9.767m/s², not 9.8m/s². In actual experiments, the acceleration of objects measured is 9.8m/s². Therefore, the centrifugal acceleration measured is???"

"Zero?" another attendee answered, sounding quite unsure of himself.

"Zero! Bravo, Mister Powers! Meaning???"

Nathan spoke up. "The Earth does not spin!"

"Correct! Well said, Mister Benton!"

"So, what about gravity? Let's talk about it. An unproven myth, a mere rumor spread around the world over the past centuries by Helio-centrists, like Copernicus, Galileo, Kepler and Newton. The Copernican theories that the Sun is at the center of the Universe, and the earth and planets revolve around it.

"This morphed into the belief that the earth is spinning around like a top, and the solar system is revolving around the Sun, which revolves around the Milky Way Galaxy. And to top it off, the whole universe is accelerating at over two million miles per hour."

Professor Thompsen leveled his eyes around the room.

"But man has witnessed the same stars in the same patterns and locations for thousands of years. Polaris, the north star at the center. Impossible on a globe, right? One word, gravity, explains their lack of true science. Gravity does not exist. What we observe is density and buoyancy."

The professor held up a globe model of the earth then let it go, allowing it to crash to the ground. It rolled into an aisleway, rousing some students to laughter.

"So, the globe I dropped is heavier than the air around it. That's it. A helium balloon or butterfly can float because they are more buoyant than their surroundings.

"This is the formula that dispels the theory of gravity." With blinding speed, he wrote out further mathematical equations.

Spontaneously, the students clapped and cheered. "That's it!" or "I get it!" and "Makes perfect sense!"

One fellow close to Nathan stood up with his pencil in the air. "Game over, Globe trotters!"

As the class ended, one student raised his hand. "Professor, is it true that Freemasons started NASA and have promoted the Heliocentric globe model for control?"

The question started a barrage of class commentary with different ones speaking up.

"It's not only the Mason's. The United Nations and governments worldwide are involved."

"Humph! Them and the bankers and the Rothchild's for sure!"

"They have been trying to crack the dome for years!"

"They're running secret underground bases, like out at Area 51."

Finally, Professor Thompsen pursed his lips, giving a loud whistle to silence the group.

"We have to wrap this up, but I challenge you to find out

more before our next symposium. Memorize the formulas for density and buoyancy and the curvature of a sphere."

On their way out of the meeting room, several students took turns kicking the globe model in the aisleway, little more than a hard useless ball.

Wasting no time, Nathan took the challenge by Professor Thompsen to heart, memorizing formulas. His aim was to expose the truth behind the spinning earth deception and be able to convince others of it, maybe even his stubborn sister.

At the University library the next day, Nathan researched how the Freemasons had partnered with governments to promote Space, NASA, The Big Bang and Darwin Theories, and the Globe model to deceive the masses worldwide.

They wanted sole control of those with the knowledge of a true encapsulated Level Earth.

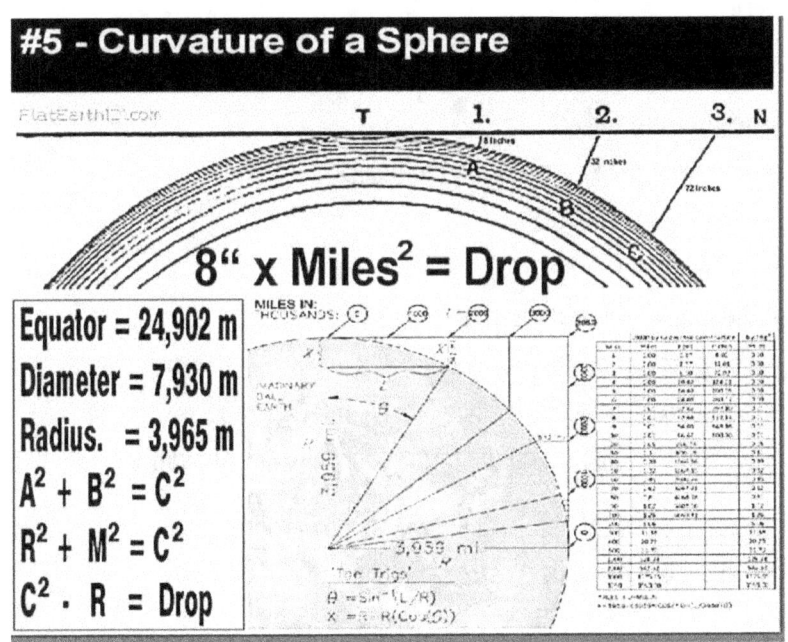

Density and Buoyancy

It's well known that gravity does not exist: how can be helium-balloons, birds, clouds or even airplanes up in the sky? It's easy to understand that the force which „decides" what is on the ground and what is flying is not this one: $F_g = mg$

Then what? I think this equation down is the correct, and yes, it doesn't contain gravity:

$$F = m\frac{c_0}{c_a + (h^2 \cdot 10^{-6})} - \rho\left(\frac{c_0}{c_a + (h^2 \cdot 10^{-6})}V + \frac{v^2 c_L A}{2}\right)$$

where

m – mass of the object

h – height from surface

ρ – **density** of the space around the object

V – volume of the object

v – true airspeed

A – the area of the wing (zero if there's no wing)

c_0 – constant of density (universal): ~398 m³/s²

c_a – constant of effective surface (air: N_2 and O_2): ~40,5 m²

c_L – Reynold's number and the form of the wing for **buoyancy.**

If the force > 0 N than, the object will stay on ground, and when it's < 0 N it will fly. You're welcome.

They wanted sole control of those with the knowledge of a true encapsulated Level Earth. With the information came a vast wealth of resources from government coffers and lands such as the Antarctic regions, circling the earth and off limits to all others.

In an obscure book, he discovered an old thesis someone had written on the Masons and one of their 33-degree leaders, chilling information indeed. How did those men get away with the things they did?

Nathan wanted to verify it, but most the information he sought—held secret—had been scrubbed from the online platforms. Search engines seemed mute on the subject. Wow.

In one of the library aisles, he caught sight of his new friend, Myiah, placing books on a cart back onto the shelves. She worked there?

The beautiful girl flashed a broad smile. "So nice to see you again, Mister Nathan."

"Yes, you, too." His faced warmed. Oh, he hoped it wouldn't get too red.

"Are you needing any help to find something?" Myiah came around the cart and stared at his notes. At the top of the page, True History of Freemasonry.

"Maybe, I'm not locating many books on this subject."

"Follow me, please." Myiah left her cart and headed down another aisle. A moment later Nathan stared at a trophy she had placed in his hands.

"Myiah! This is exactly the book I needed." He took her hand, covered it with his other and squeezed it gently. "Thank you so much. Let me buy you a coffee in appreciation."

"That isn't necessary. Just doing my job."

"But you've saved me no telling how much time, if I could have ever found it at all."

"I don't drink coffee."

"Tea, then. Do you like tea?"

"I do." She grinned. "I will have tea with you, Mister Nathan. Will you come here at five tomorrow afternoon to pick me up?'"

"I will. It's a date!"

Nathan devoured the book and once back in his dorm, wrote his report.

'Albert Pike, a known Luciferian and Freemason Grandmaster, in 1871 wrote down his plans for Three World Wars which would bring about their Luciferian New Order.

The Third would be instigated by the agents of the Illuminati in order to provoke the conflict between Israel and the Muslim nations as detailed in his letter in the 1800s to Mazzini.

Present day, his plan is ongoing according to his writings with the addition of the Ukrainian— Russian Proxy War and Taiwan tensions which bring a conflict between the Eastern and Western nations.

The US/NATO and the UK against Russia, Iran, Turkey, China and others.'

Is their next move digital currency, C40 Smart Cities, and so-called-alien invasions?

Are they not implementing the Masonic motto: 'Ordo ab Chao' – 'Order from Chaos?'"

Albert Pike's Letter Excerpt:
"The Third World War must be fomented by taking advantage of the differences caused by the 'Agentur' of the 'Illuminati' between the political Zionists and the leaders of Islamic World.

The war must be conducted in such a way that Islam (the Moslem Arabic World) and political Zionism (the State of Israel) mutually destroy each other. Meanwhile the other nations, once more divided on this issue will be constrained to fight to the point of complete physical, moral, spiritual and economical exhaustion...

We shall unleash the Nihilists and the Atheists, and we shall provoke a formidable social cataclysm which in all its horror will show clearly to the nations the effect of absolute atheism, origin of savagery and of the bloodiest turmoil.

Everywhere, the citizens, obliged to defend themselves against the world minority of revolutionaries, will exterminate those destroyers of civilization, and the multitude, disillusioned with Christianity, whose deistic spirits will from that moment be without compass or direction, anxious for an ideal, but without knowing where to render its adoration, will receive the true light through the universal manifestation of the pure doctrine of Lucifer, brought finally out in the public view.

This manifestation will result from the Ambassador reactionary movement which will follow the destruction of Christianity and atheism, both conquered and exterminated at the same time."

After copying the letter, Nathan continued, dictating his own commentary from a Biblical perspective.

They plan for America and any other free democratic nation not only to be weakened but destroyed before the New World Order

Totalitarian government of Revelation 13 rises out of the ashes of WW3.

The Anti-Christ will then confirm a better Peace Deal or Covenant with Israel and many nations to usher in a temporary false peace in the Middle East between Israel and the Muslim world (study Daniel 9:27). Satan and his Anti-Christ will be free to bring their order out of chaos.

Nathan paused collecting his thoughts. After the short break for a peanut butter and banana sandwich, he continued dictating aloud.

"This has all been carefully orchestrated by Lucifer to birth his One World Order and takeover God's Holy Land with a Two State Solution and the fall of the USA.

As Satan knows God plans to save a remnant of Israel—addressed in Daniel's 70th Week prophesy—yet nevertheless, Jesus will return to Jerusalem to reign for a thousand years.

Satan seeks to stop that with a final war against Christ. Hence the Battle of Armageddon, located just north of Jerusalem between the Anti-Christ and the Kings of the Earth (see Revelation 19-20, Joel 3, Zachariah 14)."

It was almost two o'clock in the morning by the time he finished wrestling with the difficult topics. Nathan opened his Bible to Psalm 91 and prayed for God's protection throughout the night.

Still wearing jeans and a T-shirt, he closed his eyes to rest them, knowing he'd had divine help discovering so much evil earlier in the library. But what was the Flat Earth connection?

Meeting Myiah was a God-thing, too. He knew it and reminded himself subconsciously of tea the next day—that day actually, at five. He couldn't forget. Myiah was so pretty and helpful and bold, confident, and intelligent. He fell fast asleep with a smile on his lips.

The following morning, Professor Thompsen held his regular weekend symposium. Big Jake was a no-show.

After more detailed discussion on the mathematical impossibility of a globe earth, the professor and several students walked across the street to an old 1950's style breakfast diner, bright with stainless steel and a black and white tile floor.

A note on the table read: *No cell phones or Wi-Fi allowed. Why? Not been invented yet! Enjoy the Jukebox instead.*

Arriving back late at the dorm, the football player surprised him, waiting out front. "Hey, Jake. Whassup, buddy?"

"Had a special team practice, so missed the special class."

"No worries—how's the math going?"

"Not so good. Listen, I've been placed on the disciplinary watchlist. If I fail math, they'll cut me from the team. So . . .if your offer still stands . . ."

"Of course, I'll help you."

"I could get you all the free tickets to the games you want to thank you."

Great, free tickets he'd never use . . . then he considered a different thank you. "How's your Bible reading going?"

"Guess I sort of got hung up in that Deuteronomy part."

"Well. I'll help. It'd be my honor—but you have to promise to do your part. To study what I give you. That's all the thanks I'd need."

"I will, I promise."

"Then I'll plan on meeting you tomorrow afternoon in the library. Say around four?"

"Sure. Thanks—see you then." Jake spun and waved back over his head, jogging away.

"Don't forget your math books!" Nathan called after him. He was going to have to hustle to get to the library by five.

On his way upstairs to his dorm room, another bright idea hit him. He could teach Jake the Level Earth Math of the Bible and apply it to his math lessons. He liked that idea.

He couldn't wait for tea with Myiah and getting to know her better.

The following afternoon while on his way back to the library to research a book or three, Nathan heard a group of students milling around the science courtyard.

Spotting Myiah, he rushed over in excitement and gave her a quick hug. "I was just headed to see you. What's all the commotion about?"

"I only work half-day today, but you have not heard?" she asked.

"Guess not. What?"

"Professor Thompsen! He got fired this morning!"

"Fired?"

"Given to a leave? Does that not mean fired?"

A petite redheaded girl standing nearby, chimed in. "Placed on administrative leave. I heard it had something to do with some secret Flat Earth group he was running off campus."

Chapter Seven

"Behold He cometh with the clouds and every eye shall see him."
Revelation 1:7

Early in the morning, Russ received a call from an old church friend, formerly with NATO and Military Intelligence.

"Hello?" He answered as softly as possible so as not to wake Sue.

"Russ? It's Ramos."

He moved slowly, navigating his way out of the small RV bed. The two men had communicated almost monthly since they had both retired, but he never called so early.

At the Pentagon, then Ambassador Ramos had covertly kept tabs on the 'controllers' and 'Masonic cronies' as he called them—involved in so many areas of the government.

Too many of the Pentagon luminaries were sold out to the plans for a new world devoid of faith, morals, and individual freedoms.

"You know I was right when I said the term 'military intelligence' was an oxymoron."

"For sure."

"Some of the rank and file are well intentioned though.

Where are you and Sue? Far from the big city, I hope."

Russ wasted no time taking his friend's warning seriously. "Why? What's coming?"

"Listen." An urgency enveloped his voice. "I don't like to talk about these things over the phone. I'll set you up with a secure message center and send it from there. Be watching for it."

"Will do. Thanks, Ramos."

Before long, a text came in over Telegram with a special email address. Russ opened an account posthaste and retrieved the message. Later, at a mountain retreat campground, he and Sue processed the call together.

The wooden picnic table set on the edge of the ridge, providing breathtaking views of the vast valley below. A sign read: *"It's the Pretty Place."* It obviously distracted his wife.

"Goodness, do you think we can see for fifty miles?"

"Could be." He figured she'd want to get her easel out to paint the scene, but her concern turned instead to Gwen and Nathan.

"So, Ramos mentioned contacting Gwen about a secure meeting? What was he talking about? Did he say? Why would she need a secure meeting?"

"I'm sure it's over the story she's working on. He'll coach her on how to share the information safely."

"And in the meantime, we're supposed to stay out of the cities? What about Nathan?"

"I don't think he's in any immediate danger. It's more the oil fields in Oklahoma and northern Texas."

"Why the oil fields?"

"Sounds like they're planning another destructive weather event like the firestorms in Lahaina and Paradise, California. They want a net zero-based carbon world, without cars that run on gas."

"But I read coal is used to make the batteries for the electric cars. Are they crazy? The article said they use little children in the African cobalt mines. It's pure slavery." Sue shook her head.

Russ reached out to comfort her, taking her hand. "Sounds like they plan a super cell system with multiple tornadoes to disrupt the oil supply. We're to stay miles away from the cell towers, too."

"Why?"

"Supposedly, they'll be sending nationwide signals, but at the appointed time, blast three strong microwave radiation signals at 18gh, on top of it all.

"The report shows it'll be repeated periodically with signals directed to those in opposition to their agenda. It's a damaging frequency, Ramos mentioned it being disorienting, especially to those who have the toxins and graphene oxide in them."

"You mean from the shots?"

"Most likely—but they've sprayed the skies with toxins for years."

In the distance were two large planes, spraying chem-trails, appearing to target a populated area below. Right on cue. He leaned over and gave her a gentle, reassuring kiss.

"Don't worry, love. Why don't you get out your supplies. I know you want to paint this magnificent vista before us—except for those man-made chem-clouds over there."

"I'll leave those out of it. I was thinking about it. How can anyone behold such beauty and not believe in God and give Him glory?"

He only shrugged and got up to help her with her easel and whatever else she needed him to carry. Her paintbrush always painted stress and tension right away—since childhood, her mother claimed.

His wife's artwork hung in many homes of family and friends and a few galleries, too. Adept in oils, acrylics, and watercolors, she had a God-given gift.

That evening, she captured the sun on canvas moving away from their point of view and observed how it skid slightly to the right during its descent.

"According to Nathan, the streaming light at angles would be impossible if the sun were really two million miles away."

"That's a thought." While Russ hooked up the campground services for the RV, he enjoyed watching her paint the colorful sky. He walked closer.

"It becomes smaller, as it moves away from our perspective, doesn't it?" He patted her shoulder. "Another beautiful painting, sweetie."

"They should call it 'sun-away' instead of sundown." She smiled.

The next morning on the East Coast, Gwen had a fortuitous call from her Uncle Tomas and Aunt Jan, who actively worked to expose Big Pharma. She never expected them to be the ones to get involved in political activism on such a grand scale.

When their daughter died days after a Covid shot, they immediately took to the frontlines exposing the Pharma lies.

Gwen deeply loved Cassie. She couldn't believe she'd been required to have the experimental injection to attend U.C.L.A.—the same University Nathan attended.

The very thought of it gave her a sickening feeling in the pit of her stomach. Thankfully, the mandate had been lifted before Nathan enrolled.

Auntie Jan had called her directly asking her to interview them for a Sunday evening news report. Excitedly, she agreed making the arrangements to meet them midway at Grandpa's oceanside cottage.

He'd asked her to look after the place while he sailed around the world . . . or was it better referred to as the circle of the earth? Anyway, she could kill two birds with one proverbial stone, so . . .

Her network would frown on such an expose, so she planned to film the interview for her own program and upload it online. Hopefully, her new notoriety would help with views.

She wanted to honor her cousin in any way she could. She never had a chance to say goodbye. The vibrant twenty-year-old, Cassie, had died alone in the hospital on the same night she was admitted.

The hospital barred family from visitations due to the Covid Protocols from the CDC. Not even Auntie and Uncle could go in. As an investigative journalist, Gwen also wanted to honor her grieving aunt and uncle. The interview would give her that opportunity.

She arrived early, checked out the place, then got everything ready, including the portable cameras in place and the teapot on. When they arrived, she was ready to go and took her seat.

"How did all of this start for you two?"

"After our daughter died suddenly—we knew in our hearts it was a result of the mandated Covid injection—we had to do something." Aunt Jan choked back tears. "I spiraled into my grief, but discovered it helped to share our Cassie with the world and warn others."

Uncle patted her hand, lovingly. "We dropped everything else we were doing to expose the truth about the deadly shots."

"And you've gained some notoriety on TV, haven't you?"

"Yes, some, but most of our efforts have been censored." Jan dabbed at her eyes. "We've been threatened and persecuted after almost every show, but we will not give up."

"How sad. I'm so sorry you're having to go through that." Gwen sat back in her chair and shook her head in empathy. "So tell me then, Mister Benton, how did all this morph into exposing the harmful Electro-Magnetic Frequencies, the EMF coming from the 5G Cell Towers?"

"It all started hiking at the Bonaire Gardens Park one morning. We experienced headaches, looked around, and noted a huge new cell tower only about a hundred yards from us."

"Immediately, we left the area. Within minutes both of us felt better again." Aunt Jan wiped her forehead. "I can't believe what they are doing to us."

Uncle took over for his distressed wife. "After this, we found data that connected the Covid injections and proliferation of all the new 5G towers. We moved from the west to east coast, so we could lobby Congress."

Gwen referred to her notes. "Let's see . . . So, within days, you were leading the action to lobby in Washington D.C. against all the experimental pharmaceutical injections, and then the wireless radiation, convinced both caused untold harm to many of the unwary worldwide. Is this right?"

"It is, Miss Sharpe."

"And with the cell towers, you lobbied to ensure local governments would determine where the wireless facilities are placed within the municipality to protect the public?"

"That's correct. We're just two of the millions of Americans with electromagnetic sensitivity. It's also known as microwave syndrome." Jan took in a deep breath.

"People with microwave syndrome develop symptoms such as dizziness, insomnia, pain, and mood and memory problems whenever they're exposed to electromagnetic fields—EMFs—from many power sources and wireless signals transmitted by phones, cell towers, and emerging small cells."

Her aunt held up a graphic chart showing photos of several menacing looking towers. "We noticed wireless facilities, especially small cells, started popping up like mushrooms, at the beginning of the Covid lockdowns, in both residential and commercial areas."

"There are two types of wireless facilities." Her uncle took over explaining the technical part. "Cell towers, or macro cells, can reach two hundred feet in height, may have up to twenty antennae, and maintain coverage for miles of radius.

"Small cells, on the other hand, are much more compact, and they relay signals and maintain coverage between a few hundred yards and up to about two miles.

"Though their frequencies overlap with 4G, 5G signals, they have a higher upper frequency, making them less penetrative. Therefore, they need antennae at closer proximities to maintain connections."

"I did not know all this."

"Apart from emitting 5G signals, small cells also emit 3G and 4G signals—both shown to be harmful. This means residents nearby are exposed to denser and stronger wireless radiation, increasing potential health risks."

Uncle Tomas looked into her camera with great concern in his eyes. "These are close. Global positioning satellites are a lie. Just like cell and TV signals. GPS is triangulated between towers from the ground."

Gwen digressed. "Does this have anything to do with the shape of the earth?"

Tomas paused and seemed to carefully consider his answer. "It isn't really my area of expertise, but I do know space and orbiting satellites are not what they tell us—tower signals travel for vast distances in a straight line."

"Are there any studies that bear these findings?"

With an odd expression, Aunt Jan steered the discussion back to documenting the 5G frequencies and signals with their adverse health effects. Holding up another report, she picked up where her husband left off.

"One retired oncologist, Dr. Lennart Hardell from Orebro University Hospital in Sweden, published three case studies involving residents living near a newly installed 5G small cells or base stations.

"Previously healthy people often develop symptoms of fatigue, insomnia, tinnitus, distress, skin disorders, tingling hands or feet and irregular blood pressure—this is right after a nearby 5G tower or relay station goes up."

Uncle picked up the pace. "Dr. Hardell found that after the new base station was installed, the strength of the radiofrequency signals increased. Due to the severity of symptoms, one couple left their home and moved into a small office room with lower radiation strength.

"Within a couple of days, most of their symptoms were either alleviated or disappeared completely, according to Dr. Hardell."

"So, they continue to roll out more cells? Why?"

"The 5G rollout. Smaller cells went in all over the place. Our friends have discovered them outside their homes on lamp posts and utility poles along the sidewalk. One girl we met was bleeding from the scalp after a tower was placed in her cul-de-sac."

Glancing up from his notes, her uncle nodded. "Her dad died soon after from lymphoma cancer, and her best friend across the street had a late-term miscarriage. In 2020, with

Covid killing people everywhere, they installed over four hundred seventeen thousand wireless facilities."

"What? How is it no one knows this?"

"Humph. Now there are literally almost three million of the deadly towers. We believe that the wireless towers were first designed as a weapons system. They were possibly also made for connecting the people who took the shots."

"Connecting them? What do you mean connecting them? To what?"

"Connecting them to the grid."

"Wait—what?" Gwen couldn't believe what she was hearing. "The grid? So you're saying the injected people are receiving electromagnetic signals directly from EMFs that . . . that . . . control them?"

"Affect them, control them, or worse. We have evidence that many of the unwary who were jabbed are even emitting blue tooth signals. When we expose this evil agenda and truth about it, we are labeled conspiracy theorists."

"The satellites circling in space are also a myth."

"A myth?"

"Most likely just attached to weather balloons." Jan glanced at her husband for support.

"Nothing is in geocentric orbit thirty-five thousand kilometers out in space as they would have us believe." Uncle nodded. "It's a ruse, Miss Sharpe. Based on mainstream science and NASA's own data, thermospheric temperatures increase with altitude due to absorption of highly energetic solar radiation."

Aunt Jan jumped in to explain. "My dear husband was an educator for many years. He's saying that there is no way any craft—manned or unmanned—is orbiting earth out in space. Why? Because the solar radiation would melt them."

"What advice is there for limiting the EMF exposure then?" Gwen was beginning to take the message to heart.

"Move away from cell towers." Auntie glanced at him.

"At least two miles away." He added. "Shield cell phones, equipment, and turn the routers off at night."

Holding up a baseball style cap, Jan laughed. "Listen. People are going to call you 'Tin Foil Hat Conspiracists' anyway. Might as well wear one. This hat is lined with an EMF protector." The inscription on the cap read, 'Covered by God.'

Since Gwen waded into uncharted territory with this startling data and line of questioning, she thought it best to wrap things up, before it heated up even further.

Ending the interview, she almost slipped up saying, "I want to thank my dear Unc—" Catching herself mid phrase, she cleared her throat. "To thank this courageous couple who want nothing more than to help others by sharing their heart-wrenching story and shocking information."

With the help of her techy brother, Nathan, the video quickly garnered a half million views . . . Far less than the number of cell towers deployed across the country.

That night Gwen gave a quick call to her brother to thank him for the live feed recommendation and filled him in on the 5 and even 6G radiation poisoning.

"Maybe it's like HAARP in Alaska."

"Do you think I know what that means, Nathan? What it is? My brain is so overflowing, I may have a breakdown any minute—probably from all the cell towers."

"Sorry, Sis. It's a five-mile-long grid of weaponry. For years, they have been shooting harmful frequencies around the enclosed earth dome. Scientists say it is the Ionosphere, but it's the dome.

"They tried blasting their way through it with nuclear bombs years ago—they called it 'Operation Fishbowl'—but God made the firmament impenetrable."

"Hey, what about the Tower of Babel when Nimrod tried to reach up to heaven with their evil army?" Gwen loved connecting modern day things back to the stories in the Bible.

"Nimrod was a Nephilim giant. Everyone knew about the dome earth shape back then, but the Lord scrambled their communications. You know the story, no longer one, but many languages to thwart man's evil."

"Seems like the Fall of Babylon may be here again."

"Maybe you need to start your own channel." Nathan encouraged her. "Maybe you can do something on God's true Flat Earth dome covered creation." He offered a big smile on her video call.

"Sure—that's what I'm going to do. Put an end to my network career. We'll talk later, Brother."

Later that night, a cryptic text from an unknown number lit up her cell phone.

'For your own safety, forget about the Kubrick story.'

That same night in the dorm, Nathan experienced another amazing dream. One that brought him to much prayer and introspection to discern its meaning.

Waking late for class, he dressed quickly and grabbed his backpack, heading out the door. On his way at a brisk pace, he dictated the dream in detail, holding his cell phone outward.

"I was on campus and intuitively knew that I was enrolled as one of the only students who professes faith in God.

89

Hearing the loud sound of cheering, I follow the noise down a winding path, and around the corner, see a large stadium. It was deafening. Standing away from the throngs of students lining up to enter in one line and all others entering through another set of doors, I noticed a small white door.

Opening it, I entered a long hallway into a locker room where a few football players were donning their uniforms.

A man suddenly said to me, "You're late!" He hands me football gear. "Quick! Put it on," he says. "You might miss the kickoff!"

He begins to help suit me up into the uniform. Helmet, shoulder pads. It resembles armor. He cinches the belt tight and hands me cleats.

"All I have is my t-shirt that I'm wearing," I say. "I need a jersey!"

Standing in the sunlit doorway to the field is another man. It's blinding to look straight at him because a bright light shone on him.

Or was it shining right through Him?

All around us were streaming rays of light. Loud sounds emanated from the outside, however, were then suddenly melodious.

"Come," he told me with such graciousness.

Guiding me to the field he simply says, "When it comes in your direction, you will know what to do. Wait—It will come to you."

The players are lined up on the field now in front of me. Thousands cheer in cacophony, making it difficult to hear anything. Standing with my back to the goalposts, it dawns on me that I'm a special team's guy.

Another player is on my right, yelling. "Remember if you catch the kickoff, run behind me. I'll block for you and vice versa!"

He begins to scan the sky for the ball that has been kicked in our direction. Instinctively, I do the same and watch the ball hanging above his head, descending toward his arms.

It descends from high in the domed stadium.

Running to assist my teammate, the ball lands in his hands. Suddenly, an opposing player hits him hard from the blind-side, and the ball skids in my direction. The football seems to be sliding by me into the endzone.

Then, everything seems to go into slow motion and time is suspended.

I have time to think.

If I let the ball go past me, it will be a touchback, and the ball will be brought out to the twenty-yard line. Or, if I jump on the ball to stop it, I will be crushed under the weight of the approaching players and lose yardage.

But it appears to be stopping on the goal line, which will keep our team deep in enemy territory.

With the only sensible alternative, I stick a right foot out to stop the ball. It bounces up from the turf, landing neatly in my arms. Cradling it like a baby, I dash behind my teammate, who is sacrificially pinned by several opposing players.

Heading towards the sidelines, one of them grabs my jersey as I run past. Spinning around, I pull free, but the ball pops up, striking me in the nose with a loud crack! Hitting between the helmet guard, large drops of blood drip on the ball.

"Keep going!" someone yells.

Now another teammate out in front blocks two men at once, allowing a clear lane to sprint along inside the horizontal line. Stride by stride, white intersecting lines rush by in a blur.

"Keep your eyes on the goal line!" I hear.

Yeah—don't look at those gigantic hulks coming from the side or chasing from behind in the dark uniforms. Pulling away, with longer strides, a pack of white Jerseys to my right is cheering me on.

Teammates and coaches on the sidelines are screaming: "Go! Go! Go!" One of the players is Big Jake!

With eyes fixed in front of me, I see them! The white goal posts!

Suddenly, I'm knocked forward as players from both teams fall on top of me.

Everything stops.

The world came to a halt.

Crushed under such enormous weight, the pain was excruciating, but I hung on to the ball.

Beneath my fingertips, I feel it, flattened along with me.

Then—I feel a tap on my shoulder. I'm being lifted up gently out of the pile of players by the one who was standing earlier in the doorway with sunlight streaming through Him—so blinding.

His features are hard to see. He's floating above then we're suspended under the circular glass dome. All the action remains frozen in time below.

"Do you see what is being held, cradled between your arms?" he asks.

Peering down at the flat ball, I see a deep earthen color with white laces. Instantly, the pigskin transforms into a beautiful brown leather Bible! The white laces turn to luminescent lettering: THE HOLY BIBLE.

As I hold up the Bible, the stadium is silent. The players are all frozen in place.

"Keep running towards the prize. Hold it tight, Nathan. Run the race,"

That afternoon, while resting in the University's gardens,

Nathan considered the dream that he hadn't been able to get out of his thoughts all day.

Well, of course, there was the connection with football in his subconscious, after meeting Jake, but he rarely watched a game.

In a bigger way, wasn't it for everyone who loves Jesus? For those who love His Word? Maybe for all who were on the sidelines, it was time to enter in, to pick up the pace and be about the Father's business.

Moving towards the goal line with haste to share the Word and do His will because the Day of the Lord approaches. He must run the race with endurance and finish well.

Note to Self: Remember to give Jake the quarterback a Bible!

In the mountain top campground, Russ had a different concern weighing on his mind. His military intelligence friend sent the warning. Ramos never mentioned when the cell towers would be activated or where the Defense Energy Weapons, the Pentagon's 'DEWS' would hit.

He advised them to head to a Hopi Indian Reservation. There, Russ was needed to decipher some cave writings at a huge archeological find.

His friend's encrypted message read: Please assist the Chief. If you leave in the morning, you will avoid the scheduled Texas/Oklahoma fires. Man-made destructive weather events. The damaging tower frequencies are also being activated in metropolitan areas

Chapter Eight

"The world also is established, that it cannot be moved."
Psalm 93:1

First signs of morning appeared over the distant mountain peaks as Russ and Sue hurriedly broke camp. They would be safer on the Hopi Reservation for the time being.

Driving five hours along a vast expanse seemed endless. Along the way, their favorite faithful Taizé music provided comfort. The couple often found peace in the silence without words.

Sue delighted with an ink pen flowing over the sketch book on her lap.

On his way to the native Americans' home, Russ recalled another journey to the Yucatan Peninsula where indigenous people lived peacefully. Pyramids aligned with Polaris and the North Star worldwide . . . only possible on a Flat Earth.

Why had it taken him so long to see?

But those people worshiped deities, false gods, or even the devil serpent at places like Giza, Machu Picchu and Chichén Itzá.

He and his wife had spent that spring on a mission trip near the archaeological site of Maya ruins in present-day Mexico, and its famous stepped pyramid, El Castillo—also known as the Temple of Kukulkán.

It displayed a unique phenomenon during the spring and autumn equinoxes. When the sun set over El Castillo's northwest corner, triangular shadows formed the outline of the Maya deity Kukulcan—the 'amazing serpent'—and it would slither slowly down the steps.

The Mayans knew about the rotating sky and level shape of the earth, but sadly embraced the serpent.

In recent years, locals were blinded by Catholicism. One Catholic church they visited in Merida had replaced an old stained-glass window with a counterfeit showing the Masonic pyramid eye of the sun god, RA!

And now the Mayan people were being uprooted by the world's largest company—Blackrock—who bought their lands, investing a billion dollars for constructing a new bullet train.

Thoughts turned back to the once great Hopi and Navajo Nations, the high desert Tribes' homeland covered an area the size of West Virgina, spanning New Mexico, Utah and Arizona.

He noticed how the picturesque scenery unfolded with the classic western landscape stretching out through arid valleys of clay and sage brush. It seemed the jagged shadowed mountain ridges—cut by the flood of Noah's time—guided them along dusty roads.

Finally, a sign appeared and then another, directing them into a pueblo region with signs of life. They had tried reaching out to Chief earlier, surprised that someone had answered a land line.

"Our Chief does not make appointments," a woman said. "Living moment-to-moment has its advantages—track down Chief de Chelly when you come."

Near a welcome area off the dusty road, Russ parked the RV in a shady resting spot. A weathered man on horseback galloped toward the driver's side.

"From Virginia?" the man asked.

"Yes, sir. That's home."

"I will take you to Chief." Spinning the large palomino towards the ridge, he waved an arm for them to follow. A moment later, the dishes and cups were rattling along inside their home on wheels.

"We're not really made for off-road." Russ lamented, bumping along the wide open plain.

"It is really flat though." Sue held on.

With the horse and rider losing them, he downshifted and sped up a bit. And then there on the side of a cliff, a man emerged from an impressive dwelling. Within minutes, he and Sue were introduced to the Hopi Chief.

"A friend of a brother is my friend." The man had chiseled features and flowing grey hair and wore an ornate brown outfit, and a silver medallion hung around his neck.

That evening they dined on a delicious fare of different roots and vegetables cooked over mesquite, in a large outdoor clay oven that would've been great for pizzas, Russ thought.

He discussed events of the times and admired how the Chief and his wife seemed to take it all in stride with ease.

"Many years ago, white men came telling us how to believe with religion. Bad men who did not practice those things they taught. We rejected it."

The furrow on the Chief's brow accentuated with the telling. "Then came a man from the Philippines who looked like us, named Palu. He did not so much tell us what to think, but helped with cleaning, cooking and painting. He taught the children to read. Then we wanted to know his God."

"Later, many here came to know Jesus." His wife smiled.

That same evening at U.C.L.A. found Nathan racing to meet Myiah at the student union for tea. Scanning the room, he spied her paying at the counter. Rushing over, he pulled his wallet out, but she stopped him.

"Too late. It's my treat. Hope you like Oolong tea."

After being seated, she opened up about her escape from Myanmar. "You hear of the Burmese Rangers?"

"They rescued people in your country, right?"

"Yes. They lived in tree houses hidden deep in the jungle, so not apprehended by the authorities. Living over the border in Thailand, they would bring Bibles and medical supplies and food.

"The Rangers helped natives in my area who do not follow the evil communist." Her eyes suddenly glistened with tears.

"One night, they sneak across border and rescue many in my village. The communists were coming the next day to kill all of us. We prayed, and God send them to save us."

"That's an incredible testimony, Myiah! More people need to hear it." He shuffled his feet as he often did. "It seems America has embraced too many communist ideas. It's rampant across the country, unfortunately."

"Big also in educational places, I think…"

Back in his dorm room that evening, Nathan wrote late into the night. He had come up with a Title. The heading of his manuscript read: "The Bible Never Lies – It's a Flat Earth."

His latest entries seemed the most powerful yet.

How will I ever share a Dome Earth so out of the norm?

"Is it End times?" Myiah had asked the Humanities professor.

Researching the books of Daniel and Revelation, Nathan considered the times and seasons unfolding. Pausing to pray, he asked for the Holy Spirit to guide his writing, as if it would be published.

> The transhumanist agenda appears to be spoken of in Scripture. The plagues and beasts and fallen angels from the time of the Nephilim giants were released upon mankind. The end times certainly are all here.
>
> That even those professing believers who write about Creation vs Evolution and believe the Genesis account miss the biggest lie of all. A Nephilim that came into the daughters of men altering mankind. Changing DNA, for which God sent the flood. It's happening again. They miss God's true creation; They miss God's Stationary Earth.
>
> Even though they often obliterate the false claims of evolutionary biology and geology—in direct opposition to the Biblical narrative—they still maintain absolute faith in modern cosmology, the very thing that gave birth to the false claims of all the other "ologies" they're so articulately opposed in the first place.

Nathan closed his notebook. The Lord God had called him to spread the truth about His true dome shape of the Level Earth. To use it while sharing the Gospel message to the lost.

What he held onto most was the soon return of Jesus. Scripture made it obvious that he was coming back to a Level Earth! "Every eye shall see Him," it said, and that would be impossible on a round, ball planet.

He remembered someone said they would see Jesus on TV. How laughable. It says, "Every eye shall see Him!" There are millions of people who still have no TV or phones.

He discovered a drawing proving the impossibility of that

on a globe and studied it. How can they believe it? How do they think that can happen if the world isn't flat?

Nathan continued his writing until the break of dawn.

> And those who wail at the return of Jesus are the ones who will be caught unexpectedly like a thief in the night, taken for judgment in their sins "as in the days of Noah," just as Jesus warned His disciples. While Noah remained safe in the Ark, were not all others taken away?

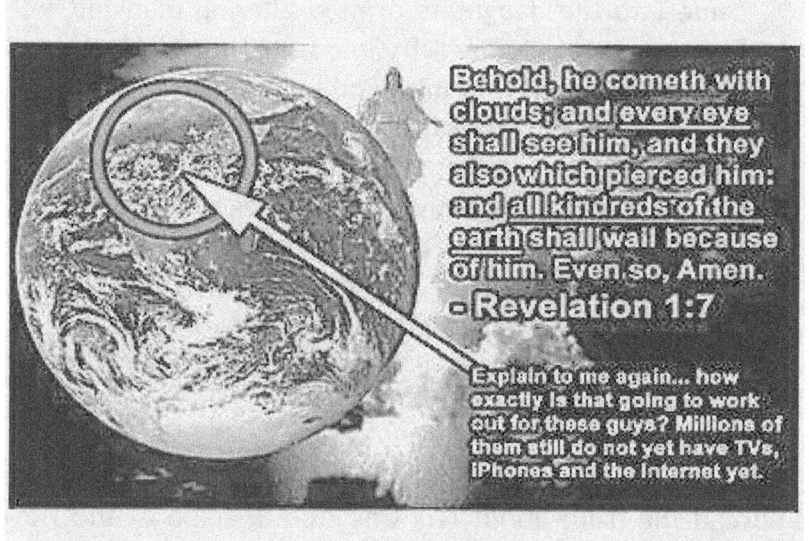

The following day, Nathan took a bus to visit his great grandmother in nearby Pasadena. At ninety-seven, Grandma Tilly still got around great. He loved her and promised Grandpa before he left on his voyage to look in on his mother.

Surprisingly, she was still quite sharp. She opened the door, and he bent to kiss her cheek before giving her a tight but gentle hug. "Grandma, it's good to see you."

"My Nathan. How's school?"

"It's fine, I guess. You sure are looking good."

"Well, living with cousin Gladys has its advantages." She winked. "I never have to take pills like they do in rest homes."

She made her way to the kitchen. Reaching over the counter, she handed him a big box of chocolates. "Dark chocolates are much better than pills!"

"I second that." Nathan laughed.

After an hour or so of non-stop visiting, he needed to get back. "Well, Grandma, I gotta go. I'm heading to a football game tonight on campus."

"Wait." She spoke in a hush, clutching Nathan's hand tightly. "Just so you know, Grandson, I believe Jesus is coming soon."

"I believe you're right, Grandma."

With the Santa Ana winds picking up, Nathan made his way through the evening air towards the campus stadium, following the sounds. It would be a first for him, and he looked forward to it.

Mainly, he wanted to make good on his promise and hand Big Jake a Bible after the game. Tutoring with 'Level Earth math' had worked well. Jake's grades had improved considerably over the two months.

Inside the stadium, he found himself watching the large screens for closer detail. Jake had given him tickets right near the field, so much of his view was blocked. With his mathematical mindset, Nathan quickly digested team statistics on his cell phone.

It was the fourth quarter, and their home team was leading by three touchdowns.

Evidently, U.C.L.A. was undefeated. Ten wins, one tie and no losses. At one-point, Big Jake was warming up on the sidelines. He glanced over at Nathan once, but never made it into the game.

Gazing up at the bright sky himself, Nathan thought about all the stadiums around the world that were covered in a dome. Sort of a picture of God's firmament creation . . . a Hemi, meaning 'half a sphere' equals a dome or the firmament.

Roars from the crowd interrupted his thoughts. U.C.L.A.'s

team was headed to the Rose Bowl. The Pac 10 championship game would be held in nearby Pasadena in two weeks.

After the game, Nathan made his way through throngs of people pressing in around the players on the field celebrating. Finding Jake, he handed him the Bible.

"In a brown paper bag?" Big Jake laughed over the crowd noise. "Your girlfriend found me one at the library yesterday."

"Girlfriend? You mean Myiah? We're just friends."

"My man, she's a girl, and she's your friend. Why not? I mean she's very nice and pretty, too."

"I agree, I do, but we just . . . uh . . ."

Another player jabbed his side. Jake grabbed the player's arm. "Hey!"

The guy was off in a flash and he turned back to Nathan, leaning over. "Just saying, I think she really likes you."

On the far side of the sea, Sam Benton awoke to a glorious sunrise. After a rough couple of days and nights of sailing, he finally had a little time and peace to act on the note from his grandson he had found in a shirt pocket.

It directed him to a book titled *Sailing Alone Around the World*, by Captain Joshua Slocum. Nathan had hidden the book aboard the Juggernaut in the galley. Sam went searching, but it didn't take him long to discover the hiding place with a hint like "coffee." With gift in hand, he climbed the stairs.

He couldn't imagine anything better than coming topside in the morning and smelling the fresh salt air with a fresh cup of coffee and a good book.

Stretching his arms upwards, he took in a deep breath, with a big yawn then hoisted the Spinnaker sail in the calm weather. *Best I catch any wind at all coming this way,* he reasoned.

While peeling the cellophane paper from the cover, an envelope dropped onto the wet teak floorboards. He quickly retrieved it, tore it open, and fanned its contents to help it dry.

It was a note from Nathan, well, more than a note, a nice three-page letter. That boy was something else. What a thoughtful kid. His heart swelled with the knowledge his only grandson really cared about him, loved him.

In the letter, Nathan poured his heart out, recalling summers spent with Sam and Sandra, and days on the beach at their Long Island cottage. It went on and on, not only bringing Sam a message of love, but sharing his faith.

He expounded on how much he appreciated those roots being established in the family, and credited Sam. How the seeds had been planted in his own father when Grandpa had served in the Navy as Chaplain.

He hadn't realized how much influence that time had on his son, Russ. His eyes watered. Here was his grandson, his wise and full of faith Nathan, bragging on him, teaching him.

The letter spoke of the boy's belief in the Biblical creation and Level Earth model. *'You surely must have seen it now, Grandpa, sailing . . . so tell me, Flat Earth or Round Globe?'* he'd written. The message ended with a slight admonition.

I implore you, Grandpa, just re-read the book of Genesis about the firmament and Isaiah about how the earth is firmly established and stationary, made in a circle and surrounded by the ice walls, all covered by a dome. Open your heart back up to God and his message for you and turn back to Jesus.

Sam re-read the letter a couple of times, tears falling down his cheeks. Scanning the far horizon and paying better attention, he considered the vast beauty, and the power of God's might that brought him through the storm.

Sipping on the cooling java now, he perked up remembering those times of studying Scripture and reading it to his expectant family—his wife filled with faith and love, Russell and Jan, in grade school then.

He remembered his son asking, "Why would Jesus take a cat-o-nine tails, to the money changers in the temple?"

Just then it donned on him.

There wasn't even a Bible aboard ship.

Now that was something to be sad about.

Chapter Nine

"Hast thou with Him spread out the sky, which is strong and as a molten looking glass?"   Job 26:7

At dawn, Sue awoke to the sound of a horse neighing loudly outside the RV. Still lying in bed, she reached up and slid open the rear curtain. There stood the Chief holding the reigns of three horses.

"We better get a move on." Russ wiped his eyes. "He's taking us out to the dig—that's one of the main reasons Ramos asked us to come. Ought to be plenty interesting, too."

Within minutes they loped out of the village over the damp trail towards the rocky mountain ridge. The morning sun shone bright accentuating the crags and pinnacles in the shadows. "Dazzling. It's *refracted sunlight*," Russ muttered.

Sue loved being on the back of a horse again. She remembered fondly taking Gwen and Nathan riding when they were children.

More recently, she had hoped for horses at their small ranch in Virginia, but that hadn't worked out . . . yet. Riding up alongside her husband, she dropped the hint. "What do you think, sweetie? Maybe we need a couple of these grand creatures back home."

"Thankful they use saddles." Russ bumped along holding

the reigns tightly in two places in a feeble attempt to control his rambunctious stallion. Glancing at her on her smaller, well-behaved gelding, he laughed.

"Maybe we should switch before I get tossed."

Overhearing their conversation, the Chief grinned.

"It has been many moons since your last ride." Bending over, he grabbed the reigns of Russ' horse and demonstrated a proper hold. "Not so tight—Silver Son knows the way."

As the party climbed higher, the open plains turned to a narrow rocky channel that ended at a dark cavern. Retrieving a large flashlight from his saddlebag, the Chief motioned for them to dismount.

He and Sue followed his unspoken example and tied their horses to a jagged pole of petrified wood.

Moments later, he found himself deep in the cave, trailing the Chief's light. Thankfully, a natural skylight also soon appeared above. Rays of sun broke through and lit the path.

Suddenly the Chief stopped and pointed out the dig with his flashlight. Squatting, Russ' heartbeat increased its effort, pumping so he could feel his pulse. The scale of the find . . .

Simultaneously, he brushed away some dirt from a rock revealing an overly large skull with its torso, legs, and feet all intact. "Chief, it's . . . this is amazing."

"One of the Anunnaki." The Native shook his head. "Our ancestors had to deal with this race."

"But it must be over ten feet tall, It was a giant." Sue moved in closer.

"There are more." The flashlight shined on several more areas with mounds and the outline of huge skeletal remains. "And something our friend asked me to show you."

Climbing up an old wooden ladder, the Chief shined the light into several smaller caverns. "It's this one to the left." Pointing the light at Russ, he went on. "It would not be right for me to move it."

On his descent, he signaled Russ to the ladder so he could see the contents of the opening. He complied, grabbing the offered flashlight on his way up, then wiggled his way into the smaller cave.

He spotted it partially uncovered, a tablet of stone. Carefully, he lifted it from its resting place and blew off the dust. The thing was heavier than he expected, but he continued until it was completely freed.

Studying it, he ascertained it to be close to a foot in width and maybe three inches thick, He held the stone with both hands, and edged his way back onto the ladder.

One rung at a time, he slowly descended, facing forward. The Chief and Sue both reached out to steady the ladder. At the bottom, he held the treasure out in their direction.

"It looks like an ancient Cuneiform Tablet and appears to bear inscriptions regarding this giant race."

"Oh, wow, Russ! This is spectacular." Sue's eyes widened, studying the drawings on the tablet.

"You will take this with you." The Chief paused, staring intently at him and his wife. "It would not be right for our people to have it or touch it due to the conflict. Remember— it belongs to God. He entrusts this sacred tablet to you."

In Manhattan, Gwen's phone's intercom lit up. "Get in here" Roger's curt message demanded. Rising to make her way to his office, she sighed. What did he want with her this time?

"I've had it with these Network cronies, Gwen." He paced around his desk. "Planning to air a new program this week. We're calling it *LATE-NIGHT LIVE, with Gwen Sharpe and the Cover Up Report."*

Wow, could it be true? Boss was finally going to buck his superiors and let her report the truth?

The first broadcast was an explosive expose' on the Freemasons and their connection with the country's space program. She interviewed several NASA insiders and former Freemasons.

Several officials gave anonymous interviews, fearing for their lives should their identities be discovered. After reviewing the content matter, the Network issued only one directive:

Any mention of a Flat Stationary Earth, or its comparison, is strictly forbidden.

On the studio set, a man hidden by the dark lighting testified. "NASA was run by the former Nazi, Werner von Braun, a man beholden to the US government for secretly importing him into the country via Project Paperclip.

"Astronauts were all either Freemasons or their sons sworn on their lives to keep the secrets they are entrusted with."

"So, you are implying, knowing what we've discovered about that secretive organization, that no one can trust NASA?"

"Why on Earth would anyone trust NASA? The moon landing was an obvious hoax. They used the same film equipment and widescreen technology director Stanley Kubrick used in his movie, *2001*. Even today, they admit to only being able to go into the low earth orbit and to losing all the telemetry data supposedly used for the moon flight."

The dark profile changed to a different man, one of the former astronauts Gwen interviewed earlier. "I resigned due to all the lies and deadly tactics."

"Deadly tactics?"

"In 1967, then government inspector Thomas Baron testified before Congress that NASA and the Apollo program suffered failures at every level. Six days after his testimony before the Congressional investigators, he died along with his wife and child. Their vehicle got pushed onto the tracks of an oncoming train."

"I'd certainly call that pretty deadly! How awful!" Gwen sat back in her chair. "Are you aware of any other evidence of such deadly tactics?"

"They took the name NASA right from the letters of SATAN, minus the 'T.'

"Minus the 'T'?"

"That's right. They took the letter 'T' out for symbolism and code. That's why during a countdown before the rocket liftoff, they say 'T minus' 10-9-8-7-6-5-4-3-2-1 before 'Liftoff.' "

"And in the Hebrew language, the pronunciation of the name *Lucifer*, sounds like the word, NASA."

"Oh, wow! I did not know that." Gwen sat forward, leaning in closer to the man. "Are all of the astronauts in on this? Do you know?"

"Most—but perhaps not all. When Gus Grissam voiced concern over the problems with communications, hinting at a scam with the Apollo missions, he died three days later in a questionable fire."

"Wasn't he the one killed aboard a capsule that exploded during a routine test?"

"That's right. Those who don't play along are eliminated from the program--ofttimes in bad ways."

"Sir, that is simply horrendous! Is there documented evidence on all this?"

"In the documentary film, *'A Funny Thing Happened on the Way to the Moon,'* the three astronauts of Apollo 11 are seen in low earth orbit, figuring out how to stage a fake image of earth for the camera."

Her incognito interviewee spoke in a hushed tone.

"In the film, you can see the astronauts manipulating the shot to make it appear that they're looking at the earth from space, making it appear the earth is thousands of miles away, and that they're approaching its lunar orbit. In fact, they're not that far above the earth.

"Watchers can hear the astronauts discussing with NASA engineers on the ground exactly how to stage the hoax."

"I haven't seen that, but I'll be googling it as soon as we're off air."

"Radiation is also a problem. Supposedly, in order to reach the moon, our ships must pass through the Van Allen Radiation Belt, but the so-called belt, shown to be in the shape of a figure eight, doesn't even exist. NASA states it is one of their biggest problems, so they are confined to what they call a 'low earth orbit.' "

"A low earth orbit? Is that their roundabout way of admitting they never really went to the moon?"

"Call it what you will. It's all a sham." The former astronaut shook his head. "They cover it up by saying they lost the telemetry data needed for a return trip to the moon." His voice sounded full of disgust.

Gwen thanked her panel on the program and continued by showing footage of the crew purported to be aboard the Space Station. Video after video uncovered proven failures, using CGI green screen technology.

After a commercial break, in the follow-up segment, she reported more on the faked spacewalks, again showing videos rightly available in the public domain, of how the walks were filmed at a Houston underwater facility.

"Viewers, please note the tiny water bubbles shown in the darkened footage. Those are escaping from their space suits. They are not in space, only underwater. In the helmet glass, pay special attention, and you can see the clearly visible reflections of the cameramen filming the deception."

As the program ended, she took great care in revealing the names of the many Masons involved in the scientific shams over the years, beginning as far back as Galileo, Newton, Copernicus, and Kepler.

"Many more recent names, quite recognizable, including U.S. Presidents, industrial moguls, and those known in the high-tech fields have been Freemasons. Walt Disney was one high-level Mason involved with NASA. His legacy continues today.

"Sadly, they seek to indoctrinate our children through their films and video games." A tear formed in the corner of her eye as she looked directly into the camera.

"In the film, *Luna*, released under the Disney Pixar brand, the moon is shown very close to the earth. Characters climb up on a ladder to the passing moon, covered with fallen stars. A big star falls and lands like a pentagram, a masonic symbol."

Showing the clips of what she reported on as she went, she wrapped up the show.

"In Disney's *Chicken Little*, an alien invasion with holographic illusions are shown in the sky. Many believe these deep-state ruses may be coming to deceive the masses; a staged fake alien invasion using holograms.

"Thankfully, we believe there are still viewers who want the truth—for the truth will set them free. Where can true news be found though in this world filled with deceptions and lies? Right here. Join me nightly for *The Coverup Report*. This is Gwen Sharpe reporting."

After the program concluded, Roger gave her a big bear hug! "You are a brave woman, young lady. I'm so proud of you. We definitely have a hit on our hands!"

"So long as no one puts a 'hit' out on me—on us! It took you going up against the Network to allow me this program, and I'm eternally grateful."

One nearby producer responded with raised eyebrows.

With a guarded smile, Gwen scanned the room warily. Removing her earpiece, she waved to the technicians in the booth. As she walked off the set, several newsroom co-workers offered a smattering of applause.

Bright and early the following Monday, Roger leaned back in his oversized leather chair, passing out assignments to the news staff. Waiting until the office cleared, he held up a file in Gwen's direction.

"All right, Gwen. We're taking your nightly *Cover-Up Report* on the road this week."

"Where to, Boss?"

"Tomorrow in Dallas, one of those crazy conspiracy conferences opens its doors. I want you to be there. Ratings are through the roof with last night's report. People love this stuff. See if there's anyone down there in Texas who has some truth. Should afford some good laughs as well."

"May not be so funny, Boss. I'll see what I can find out." She hesitated. "It's possible there may be more truth than we know, with everything going on behind the scenes these days. Any kind of bodyguard heading down there with me?"

As soon as she asked, she knew none was necessary. Who could protect her any better than God's own angels? Nathan told her they were always with her and that God Himself held her in His hands.

"Just my favorite cameraman. Pepe will meet you there."

That night, an excitement filled her after saying a little bedtime prayer. She heard these words: *"I will gather you together, my children, and show you great things."*

Immediately, she reached out to her folks and her brother, hoping they might be able to meet her in Dallas for the conference. What a divine coincidence that it coincided perfectly with U.C.L.A.'s fall break.

Though it would take her folks a couple more days to travel across the southwest, they promised to head the RV south to the Lone Star State posthaste.

Nathan used the opportunity to invite his former professor to the conference, since he remained on administrative leave. Doctor Thompsen seemed excited about the trip.

"Not only will I come, I'll pay for the tickets. I'd like to invite anyone in the class who wants to attend if that's good with you."

"Absolutely, sir. The more the merrier."

"Great!" Dr. Thompsen sounded elated. "The geocentric earth book I wrote was just published. I'm going to see about a vendor's booth."

"My sister Gwen is a reporter who contacted the organizers. She mentioned knowing you through me, and they're hoping you might consider giving one of your more basic lectures. I have their number for you."

"Excellent. What do you think? One of the advanced math calculations talk?"

"Sure, anything like that—but you won't be having to hold back on anything."

"That will work. Hey—I've been watching your sister's *Cover Up Report*. It will be great to meet her. She seems like a real dynamo."

Chapter Ten

"The measure thereof is longer than the earth, and broader than the sea."   Job 11:9

The day's first sunlight in New Mexico angled through the RV window, waking Russ. A prism of color danced upon the wall above his head.

At the sound of children playing, he cracked the mini blind to see Sue dancing in a circle, holding hands with children on either side. He recognized the song she was teaching them. How he loved his wife!

"The River of Life sets our feet to dancing—with the River of Life, Jesus sets us free!"

As the strains of singing faded and he watched his wife work her way to the RV. Several little arms still wrapped her waist and little hands clung to fistfuls of her skirt.

He dressed quickly thinking they were coming inside to tour their home on wheels, but instead, Sue bent down opening the storage compartment. She pulled out several backpacks and gifted them to the children before poking her head in the RV's front door.

"Good morning, sweetie. We're just going to have a little art class with the kids in the Village Hall. The chief would like you to come and join everyone there around noon for a special event. Lunch, too, before we take off."

He spent the morning studying their new find. The Cuneiform Tablet fascinated him, made him anxious to decipher each marking to make sense of its origins and the inscriptions.

A knock on the door called for a quick glance at his watch. More time than he thought had passed. It was after twelve.

"Come on, Mister Benton." A young boy tugged at his sleeve. "Everyone is waiting. The Chief said to bring the rock with the writing on it. There's a big surprise!"

On the walk over to the hall, Russ noticed a tall slingshot protruding out of the boy's pocket.

"You pretty good with that sling? I know of a man who once killed a giant with one of those. Have you heard that story? About David and Goliath?

"Yes, sir. I know it." The boy reached into his pocket. grabbing the sling, then reached over without stopping and picked up a stone. "See that jar over there?"

"I do."

As quickly as he got the words out of his mouth, a ping sounded and the glass cracked forty feet away.

"My, my, you are good." He rustled the child's black hair, and the boy gave him a proud grin.

Entering the meeting hall, hoots and hollers greeted him as though he was some kind of hero, but he hadn't done anything special. The chief motioned for him to come forward then for Sue to join them.

Everyone got still.

"You all know of the bones in the Caves of Paterone, a great discovery for our people, and not only the skeletal remains of the ancestors' enemy." With one telling look, Russ held up the inscribed tablet of Stone.

Chief De Chelly continued. "These two brave souls helped discover another treasure. A tablet that brings light to the history of our people. Not unlike a story told in the Bible." He looked to Russ. "My brother."

"The book of Joshua tells of how the One Great God commanded the people to cross into the Promised Land and rid the country of giants. Your ancestors also engaged the giants and overcame them right here."

"Doctor Russell Benton is going to translate the stone."

"It may take a little while." Russ smiled.

Suddenly, the young boy with the slingshot came to the front, cradling a small white dog in his arms. He handed the animal to his chief.

"This is the brave little dog who fought the wolves, protected the school children. Our own Moki' came and chased them away with stones from his slingshot." Chief gave a broad smile at the boy, handing the dog off to Sue. "Our new friends will need a protector for the stone."

She petted the little dog. "Does he have a name?"

"Skah Menewa." A lady sitting in front chirped, returning his wife's smile.

"What does that mean?"

"Great White Protector!" The young boy thrust a fist into the air and shouted.

Russ reached over and scuffled the dog's head as he had Moki's. "I think the translation would be Mighty Whitey!"

As the RV pulled out of the Hopi Reservation, a line of children ran alongside. Two braves on horseback flanked the vehicle. Sue suddenly broke into tears.

"Stop, Russ. Stop the RV." She jumped out, opened the storage compartment, and began handing out the food stores and camping gear. Lanterns, cookware, folding chairs—all of it. Russ came to join her.

Climbing back into her seat, she smiled. "We can always buy more."

Arriving in Dallas for the Level Earth Conference, Gwen was shocked and delighted at the same time. Thousands in attendance meant many heard and believed.

The false globe model being smashed to smithereens by the brightest and best minds on earth attracted the masses to the truth.

Previous conferences had taken place in Florida, the Carolinas, and Denver, but none had been so well attended. Brazil, Britain, and Italy also hosted Flat Earth conventions.

Millions worldwide came to faith in the Biblical earth model.

The event's schedule resembled most corporate conferences, with some fairly notable twists. Speakers gave presentations including "Space is Fake" and "Testing the Moon: A Globe Lie Perspective."

Awards for the year's best Flat Earth-related videos were handed out, and believers reveled in the opportunity to meet and question several of the movement's most influential men and women.

In Gwen's first televised interview, one of the organizers, David Weiss, welcomed her to the platform.

"I tried for months to find proof of the Earth's curvature but failed. Discovering the earth was both flat and stationary . . . it turned my world upside down."

"How did you react, once you were convinced?"

"I absolutely freaked out. It literally rips the rug out from underneath you." He mentioned how tedious it was to associate with the majority of people who still hold fast to the lie.

"Unfortunately, I still have friends and family who believe in a round earth. People have their choices to make, and many choose to believe we live on a ball. Of course, they're wrong."

Weiss' motioned to those in the vast crowd. "This new community . . . Are you to share this life-altering belief to the world?" The crowd erupted in cheers. "Our fellow believers are spreading the truth to the four corners of the earth!"

Another event coordinator hurried to the podium. "One-in-five people are not entirely certain the world is round, while a 2019 Datafolha Institute survey of Brazilian adults indicates that millions there believe in a dome earth."

He explained how the Flat Earth community has its own celebrities, music, and merchandise along with a weighty catalog of pseudo-scientific theories.

"It's been the subject of a recent Netflix documentary endorsed by famous musicians. Each year, more Flat Earth events fill the calendar." He raised his arms victoriously amidst a melee of cheers and hoorahs.

A moment later, Gwen had the honor to introduce Professor Thompsen for his keynote address.

"All the nations of our Level Earth once believed in the stationary dome firmament model we live on." Dr. Thompsen peered out over the thousands that seemed to be hanging on his every word. Gwen thought she really could have heard a pin drop.

"We have been influenced with a false heliocentric space model. The ruse is a part of the deception of a Masonic organization with the backing of the world's power brokers. It's called NASA."

Murmurs sounded across the auditorium. Some even booed.

The professor placed a model up on the large screens surrounding the auditorium.

"Which is the only one that doesn't match up with the history of the world?"

"NASA's!" Calls resounded out from the audience.

"NASA is evil!"

"They deceive the world."

"Space walks are done in underwater tanks!"

"And they steal billions of your tax dollars," the professor added. "Let me show you a little film."

On the screen came the fake moon landing footage shot by Stanley Kubrick that Gwen had provided. It revealed the interior of a studio set with astronaut actors, lights, cameras, and wires used to make it look like men were walking on the moon dressed in spacesuits.

After a few online meetings with Professor Thompsen, Gwen had looked forward to meeting Brad at the convention. In person, she found him quite dashing. Plus, Nathan assured her he was a man of deep faith. His talk was captivating. . .

"The director who filmed the fake so-called moon landings saved this footage to prove everything was faked. In another video Kubrick says: 'Don't you think that people have the right to know the truth?' I agree.

"In the end, I believe it cost him his life according to his family. They were interviewed by a reporter I know." Brad smiled from the stage into the wing at Gwen.

"Now I know a lot of you believe everything with the moon landings was faked, and you would be right. If you refuse to believe in the false science of evolution with a heliocentric globe model, you would be right. If in response, you believe in a Flat Earth—you are absolutely right!"

At that juncture of the talk, the crowd erupted in applause. As it died down, the professor continued.

"The one thing many of you are divided about is who made you? A lot of Level Earthers still believe aliens came down and seeded mankind somehow, or even created a little caged dome model earth . . .that the beings are sitting above us like we are caged for them to study, or use our DNA, or even that we are in an alien zoo of some kind."

The professor paused and grabbed a remote for his computer. "Here is what I believe from Genesis." Appearing on the screen were Bible verses.

GOD CREATED THE HEAVEN AND THE EARTH.
GOD SAID, 'LET THERE BE A FIRMAMENT'
GOD CREATED MAN IN HIS OWN IMAGE.

"We need to come together on this one. There are over two hundred verses in the Bible that highlight a stationary, level dome model earth and explain in detail both all of its history and what is to come.

"Let me know after the conference if you want to know more about this, or just ask, and I will give you one of my books for free."

Gwen figured there had to be at least around half—if not more—there who were Christian believers. A resounding applause rang out over the room as Dr. Thompsen waved and departed the podium.

Next up was former England cricketer, 'Freddy' Flintoff. He took to the stand and admitted being obsessed with Flat Earth. He engaged the crowd asking a lot of questions.

"If you're in a hovering helicopter, why does the earth not rotate under you if it is indeed a spinning ball?

"Why, if we're hurtling through space, would water remain still? Why isn't it wobbling?

"Also, if you fire a laser horizontally one hundred miles . . . you shouldn't be able to see it if there was curvature, should you? Yet, you can." Freddy waved his arms around through the air.

"There is a global conspiracy to conceal the truth."

"Tell them about the Black Rock!" someone in the crowd yelled.

"Yeah—okay." Freddy paused as if to gather his thoughts. "Now Flat Earthers are very fond of this one!"

Laughter rippled across the auditorium.

"So, the middle of our Flat Earth is the North Pole with a vortex. The biggest mountain in the world is there; it's called Black Rock. That's where the globalist company got its name.

"Around the Flat or Level Earth's outside is the South Pole which forms a wall of ice. When discovered, twelve countries ratified the Antarctic Treaty at the United Nations in 1959 which halted private exploration.

"This is why all the governments have bases at the South Pole."

"Why has no country claimed it? If Antarctica really was a continent, and not a massive ice wall around the edge of our Flat Earth?"

As Freddy wrapped up his talk, he placed a few more points on the large screens for all to ponder.

"See you on a level playing field!"

He waved goodbye.

FREDDY'S FOUR POINTS TO PODER:

1.   Most EVERY civilization believed in the Dome and Level Earth Model until the evolutionists rewrote history.

2.   If Earth is a globe, wouldn't rivers such as the Mississippi

or Nile, have to flow uphill to reach the sea? Flowing uphill eleven miles of its three-thousand-mile length?

3. If Earth is a globe, wouldn't airline pilots have to constantly adjust their controls so as not to fly off into space?

4. If Earth is a globe, rockets should be able to fly straight up without crashing into something, right?

Nathan spent most of his time at the convention gathering material for the book he was writing based on the true-shape-of-the-earth doctrine. He wanted it to be the first published from the Bible's perspective.

That night, he called Myiah on his cell phone from a Thai restaurant. Hearing her mellifluous voice saying she missed him boosted his spirit, and after the call, her picture popped up on telegram with a heart.

Looking up from his phone, he spotted his sister being seated on the restaurant balcony outside—and Doctor Thompsen was with her! Were they like on a date? Nathan grinned from ear to ear. He sure hoped so.

He wanted to spend some time assisting her. So far, he'd done little more than introduce her to his professor. He had both been so busy though, and obviously, so had she.

Gwen spent the following morning interviewing more key Level Earthers for her nightly nationwide broadcast. Nathan helped her cameraman, Pepe, who trained him quickly on the equipment.

"Your hired!" laughed Pepe, handing him the large camera and sound gear. "I'm heading to e*l baño!*"

"I've never experienced such growth in such a short period of time." Robbie Davidson, founder of the Dallas conference, adjusted himself in the overstuffed chair. "I'd say within ten years, the numbers will be astounding. Next year, every major country in the world will be hosting a Flat Earth conference."

"And Mister Weiss, what do you think brings this community together?"

"For one thing, the conferences. It's good to shake hands, meet face-to-face, and give each other hugs. We can collaborate and make new friends of like believers, because guess what? Our old friends . . . Well, we lost a lot of them."

The conference founder spoke up again. "When I first heard people believed in a Flat Earth, I just laughed and thought they had to be the stupidest people ever. Who in their right mind could believe something so idiotic?"

Davidson chuckled. "A couple of years later, I was one of those setting up the *First International Flat Earth Conference*. After spending two years trying to prove the earth was a round ball, I finally gave up—and gave in."

"Mister Davidson, I understand you are a born-again Christian."

"That's right."

"So, could you explain to me a logical explanation for this . . . this conspiracy of the millennium?"

"Let's just say, Gwen, there is an adversary, the devil, Satan. He wants to convince the world God doesn't exist. I'd say he's been quite effective convincing people we live on a random speck in an infinite universe.

"The reality though is that the Flat Earth, sun, moon and stars are contained in a *Truman Show*-like dome. From there, pitfalls can be easily dismissed. Take the photos of the earth supposedly from space, I believe they are photoshopped.

"This all goes away if NASA put a camera with twenty-four/seven feed on the moon, doesn't it? So why don't they?"

"I . . . I couldn't say. Because they don't want to prove us right?"

"That's right. It took very little time to find a large online community believing that same thing, so decided a conference would take it to the next level.

"Perhaps cause the world to wake up and say, 'Wait a minute – something must be going on.' This isn't just some internet fad, or a bunch of crazies. Look how many level-headed people have paid to come to Dallas."

"Most importantly, none of us believe we're on a pancake flying through space. We understand space doesn't exist, not as we've been duped into believing. We know the world sits still, and the moon landing was faked."

"I've also heard Flat Earthers don't believe in gravity."

"It doesn't exist. Who has ever seen gravity?"

"So, no one will ever fall of the edge of our Earth?" Gwen smiled.

"Correct, because there is no edge. Flat Earthers' views of the world model may vary, but most of us believe the planet is a circular disk shape with an ice barrier around the edge.

"Also, we give warnings about *The Flat Earth Society*. This false organization is a government-controlled body designed to pump out misinformation and make the Flat

Earth cause sound far-fetched to curious minds. They put out ridiculous theories."

In her broadcast that evening, Gwen also weighed in on her time at the convention, after thanking her guests.

"It's hard to find a Flat Earther who doesn't believe most other conspiracies under the sun. A Flat Earth Conference is invariably also a gathering of anti-vaxxers, 9/11 truthers, and anti-Free Mason and Illuminati subscribers to name a few.

"It's that hyper-skeptical mindset that helps Flat Earthers answer the big questions like who's hiding the true shape of the planet from us? And why?"

Gwen ended the program by asking the audience a challenging question.

"The ruling elite, from the royal family to the Rockefellers, Rothschilds—all of those groups that run the world, when you research this for yourself, ask 'Are they not all in on it?"

What a draining day! Gwen returned to her suite as worn out as if she'd been shoveling concrete all day. Still, she couldn't keep a smile from creeping back on her lips.

Exposing the truth could be quite harrowing.

Her cell phone played the Hallelujah Chorus. She expected it to be Roger checking in, or her brother—she'd hardly had time to say four words to him all day—but seeing the name, her heart skipped a beat.

Brad Thompsen, she considered. *Miss-es Brad Thompsen. . .* It had a nice ring. What was she doing? Acting like a silly lovestruck schoolgirl. Still though, she had so much in common with the man . . .

And he wasn't too much older. At twenty-seven, already a full professor and author; best of all, he was a man of faith.

"Hope you like surprises." Brad sounded resolute. "Are you free early tomorrow morning for a couple of hours?"

"How early?"

"We would need to leave by six." He waited in silence while she pondered if she could be up and ready for the day so early when she was already so tired.

"I promise you'll enjoy yourself. It will be an exciting excursion you'll never forget."

"Wow, how can I say no to that?"

"Great. I'll pick you—"

"It's just the six o'clock business. I just don't know if I can."

"You can do all things through Christ, right? Consider it research for the convention."

"Oh, all right. I'll be the bleary-eyed lady in the lobby at six sucking coffee down—if there is coffee."

"Absolutely! Fruit and pastries, too. Bring a sweater or jacket."

Chapter Eleven

"And the stars of heaven fell unto the earth, even as a fig tree casteth her untimely figs. When she is shaken of a mighty wind."
Revelation 6:13

On the morning drive through the arid Texas valley, Gwen marveled aloud as the sun's rising rays angled to form a prism of colors.

"Breathtaking. The sun seems so close, and the moon is still up."

"Students have asked me why the moon is often out during the day." She'd sensed Brad gazing over her way several times. "They are close to each other. On a circuit."

Suddenly, spotting a sign with a small red balloon attached, he hit the brakes, past a row of tall oak trees, then made a sharp right turn, heading the SUV down a gravel road.

Finally slowing, Gwen raised her head to spot the mystery. Out front, a tall thin envelope looked to be being filled with gas . . . helium, maybe?

"Wait—we're not going up in that, right? Is it a hot air balloon?" The word surprise didn't tell the half of it.

"There he is!" Brad laughed, parked, and looked at her intently. "It's Professor Muldoon and his hot air balloon! I met him at the convention."

"Oh, Brad, I don't know . . . Is it safe?"

"Maybe not. I'm willing to take my chances with you."

She nodded in affirmation. Climbing into the gondola, reservations and all, she felt strong hands grip her waist, helping her into the basket. Gwen smiled back at her tall suitor. "Very nice move, Dr. Thompsen."

Once airborne, their host must have heard her arguments because he started right off reassuring her.

"I haven't had a crash in a while." Muldoon smiled, lifting the corners of the long black moustache, before breaking into a chuckle. His thick black beard had lovely silver highlights, so distinguished looking.

Throw in a cape and top hat for drama. A shock of wild hair added to the appearance of a man who might be a little bit crazy. What had Brad been thinking?

"Early mornings make for the best rides due to the still air." Brad explained. Once aloft, the gentle rocking and wide-open views surrounding her heightened her senses.

"It is beautiful, and as if we're touching the sky." Gwen reached for his hand, steadying herself on the rail with the other.

The rushing sound of helium filling the balloon envelope broke the silence: *Phhhhst, phsssht, phewww...*

"Up, up and away," Gwen whispered. "I never dreamed

"These vistas for miles on end confirmed my faith in Flat Earth." Professor Muldoon broke the mood.

"I was going to ask you about that." Gwen grinned. "Brad mentioned meeting you at the convention?"

"Well, I used to be a globe-head. Like so many, went off determined to disprove a Level Earth for years. But another balloonist took me up and pointed out while hovering up here how the earth wasn't spinning down below."

"How will we land close to where we started? Shouldn't we be hundreds of miles away after several hours of steady drifting?"

"You would think, wouldn't you?" Stretching out his arm, Professor Muldoon swept the horizon three hundred sixty degrees. His arms waving in the wind he went on.

"And obviously, there's no curve. Here, or from space. They always use those cameras with the convex lens to show the fake curvature. Here in Texas, we all know that NASA is nothing but smoke and mirrors."

"Are you a bona fide professor or a hot air ballon showman?" She couldn't help herself.

Sweeping his cape around, he bent at the waist in a low bow. "Professor of aeronautics, ma'am, at your service." He gave a hearty laugh.

They drifted in silence. Large birds danced around the woven basket. *How majestic soaring alongside*, she thought. Playing like dolphins around Grandpa's sailboat. Up below the clouds, it seemed as if time stood still.

"It's so romantic." Gwen practically cooed under her breath.

Brad smiled taking a chance. Leaning in—he gave her a light peck on the cheek.

Muldoon reached over checking the propane tanks. "Better start locating a safe place to land."

Brad weighed in, extending an arm to Gwen. "See, a balloon is not actually flown in a way where the pilot has much control on where they go or land. They are entirely atmospheric dependent."

"What does that even mean?"

"What Professor Muldoon controls is the up and down using the propane to heat up the air of the envelope to make it rise, and he pulls on the rope--or line—that releases the hot air to descend."

"Like he's doing now?"

"Just like that."

"Aren't we going to have to hike back to the cars?"

"My wife is down there. She's been following us in a van below, so hopefully she'll be nearby." Muldoon scanned the ground with binoculars. "No cell reception up here."

Aiming for an open field, the wind suddenly picked up, and instead headed them straight towards a barbed-wire fence. Scraping along the fence, the gondola finally touched down in a thick briar patch momentarily, then raised up a few feet again, still skidding rapidly across the field.

"There's a downed tree straight ahead!"

"Whatever you do, stay in the basket!" Muldoon hollered. "Remember—stay in the basket!"

Wham! It struck the log squarely, tipping over onto its side. Reaching over, Brad grabbed Gwen by both legs, keeping her from being thrown out into the air. Landing sideways on top of her, he kept her inside the basket that finally settled and stopped moving.

In his arms, Gwen's heart beat to the nines.

"Humph. You were right about one thing. This was definitely an experience to remember." Breathing a sigh of relief, she whispered a prayer. "Thank you, God, for saving us."

"You two just cozy up as long as you like…" Professor Muldoon smiled at them lying still. "As long as you like…"

The following afternoon, Gwen took to the Texas convention stage once again, interviewing a filmmaker, Mark Sargent, a stalwart in the movement. Sargent had been featured in the 2018 Netflix documentary *Behind the Curve*.

"Once you get into Flat Earth, the other conspiracy theories get knocked down into another tier."

Gwen laughed. "Yes, sir. I heard someone here say 'It's the Mother of all Conspiracies.'"

"That's true. Everybody here has their personal top ten conspiracies. If you walked around the convention asking what those were, they would differ from person to person, but everybody's number one? Always Flat Earth."

"I would think it helps that the group has a mutual target."

"Absolutely. Most of our ire points towards NASA. That's our bread and butter." Sargent smiled. "It's the agency Flat Earthers believe is ultimately behind the conspiracy these days.

"For me, Flat Earth was a binge watch on YouTube in the beginning. It's all been aided by algorithms and personalized recommendations now, turning Flat Earth research into a never-ending rabbit hole. This year, YouTube started burying videos and reducing recommendations of what they call 'borderline content.'"

"But that doesn't stop anyone here, does it?" Gwen furled her brow.

"No, ma'am. Doesn't make much difference anymore. Anything on social media is always going to be helpful if it goes viral, right?" He smiled. "Well, Flat Earth has gone viral."

"So . . . is this rapid growth of a movement rejecting what is taught as fundamental science worrying the mainstream?"

"I don't think so. Seems that increasingly, people aren't trusting scientists and experts—or their motives—like they used to. And there's a side effect to Flat Earth once you get into it. You automatically revisit any of your old skepticisms.

"It's a slippery slope when you think that the government has been lying and hiding such things. All of a sudden, you become one of those people thinking 'How can you trust *anything* on mainstream media?'"

"Mister Davidson, I was told you, planned a debate with some leading members of the scientific community, but they turned you down?"

"Yep, they mock us. At the core, they're afraid to debate because they will always lose out to the truth."

"But you're not deterred."

"Not in the least. It's touching everyone, and it isn't going away. Or slow down either. This True Level Earth is out of the can!"

The live crowd lit up in applause.

Gwen looked up from her interview through the bright camera lights and spotted her parents. They had finally arrived in Dallas.

"Don't forget to watch my *Cover-Up Report* on the tube later tonight. Many of you here will be on the show!"

Stepping off the stage, she shielded her eyes for a better view. The folks hugged Nathan and were shaking hands with someone. Gwen recoiled. It was Brad! Her parents were meeting Brad!

She hurried toward them and gave them big hugs. "I see you met Brad." He put his arm around her waist, and she grinned up at him. "These are my parents."

Her father gave an approving smile.

Nathan could not wait to tell Myiah that he was a matchmaker.

In the Longhorn Hotel lounge, Russ and Sue gathered the family to watch the Rose Bowl game being televised live. U.C.L.A. versus Stanford, and both teams were undefeated in the Pac Ten.

"My friend, Jake, is the backup quarterback but they never put him in the game. Poor guy. There he is—number twelve—warming the bench as usual."

"Nathan is tutoring him in math." Gwen smiled.

"We'll have to turn the channel during the game to catch Sis's *Cover-Up Report*. Have you been able to see it yet?"

"No, we haven't watched any TV of late—no reception." Russ shrugged to his daughter. "We've been out on the Hopi Reservation and man, oh, man, do I have something to share with the two of you!"

"And so do I." Sue butted in, bending over her big bag to reveal the newest family addition. "This is *Mighty Whitey*."

"Oh, mother! Mighty Whitey? Really?"

"There's a story behind it. I already love the little rascal so much, it's crazy." She told them how the little dog had rescued the schoolchildren and earned his Hopi name."

"Your mother is obsessed. She found this blue harness that makes him look like he's a service dog and carries him in wherever we go."

"I thought it would be better in here not to take a chance, so I brought him in his hideaway bag tonight."

"She embroidered *'Bravo Pero'* on the harness." He rolled his eyes at his wife.

"It means brave dog." She looked at him. "There's nothing wrong with that either!" She half stuck her head in the bag. "He's mama's brave doggie, aren't you, little buddy?"

Russ shared a bit of his news, saying he wanted them to see it after the game and Gwen's show.

During a commercial break, Professor Thompson directed a comment to Nathan. "Just so you know, I'm rooting for Stanford after U.C.L.A. cut me." He laughed.

"Traitor!" Nathan joined in the joviality.

The competition proved uneventful, but what else could be expected from the best two defensive teams in the country?

Tied at seven-seven going into the fourth quarter, Russ moved them out to the RV, keeping the game on, but the volume turned down, and carefully uncovered his tablet.

Doctor Thompsen seemed the most fascinated. For his daughter, Russ liked the man. He acted very attentive towards her, and she obviously enjoyed his company just as much.

"Mister Benton, you should share this with the conference."

"Oh, that would be awesome, Dad, and Brad's right. They would all love hearing this! Seeing the tablet." Gwen turned to Brad. "Can you talk to Mister Davidson and see if there's time?"

"Oh, Robbie will make time, trust me."

"I'll get Pepe to film it for me and use it on my show as well!"

"Sounds like a plan." Russ extended his hand to Thompsen and the professor shook it heartily.

Finally, going into the last two minutes, Stanford sacked the U.C.L.A. quarterback, and the trainers had to help him off the field. Miraculously, Jake went into the game!

"Let's pray for Jake." Nathan bowed his head, not waiting for the others. "Father be with my friend. Show Yourself in a mighty way to him and we'll give you all the glory. In the name of Your beloved Son, Yeshua, I ask this. Amen.".

Turning the TV's volume up, all eyes were on the small screen television. The ball got hiked back to him, but Jake only scrambled around and couldn't get a throw off. He ran out of bounds before getting clobbered.

"Maybe he needs more prayers." Sue's expression appeared worried.

The clock wound down with Jake trying to get into field goal position. A three-point kick could win it.

On the next play a wall of Stanford giants rushed at his friend. A blitz. Now he was running the wrong way towards his own goal! Suddenly, Jake spun around and searched down field for a receiver.

Shifting his body sideways, Jake hauled off with a mighty pass, releasing the pigskin only seconds before several players viciously knocked him backwards and fell on top of him.

The ball spiraled upwards, seeming to hover endlessly, making its way to the far end of the field. The crowd hushed on both sides of the stadium.

Jake's intended wide receiver jumped several feet into the air as if off a trampoline and caught the ball! He tucked it into his midsection, but his feet never hit the ground to start running again.

A defensive end from Stanford knocked him right into the endzone for a touchdown!

The stadium clock buzzed the end of the game. Zero seconds left! Jake won the game for U.C.L.A.!

Afterward, in a News Sports interview, Jake's comment swelled Nathan's heart to near exploding.

"Have to admit, I was nervous going into the game, but God gets all the credit. I'm not a Catholic, so I guess you could call it a 'Hail Jesus pass.' If I only get one play in my college football career, I'll take this one."

The following morning, as the conference would be drawing to its end, Gwen invited her father, carrying his tablet treasure, up onto the stage. Doctor Thompson introduced him.

Without missing a beat, her father explained the meaning of the Cuneiform Tablet. Nathan worked with Pepe getting the video on the big screens for all to have a better view.

"There once lived a race of giants—of Goliath's proportions—right here in the U.S. of A. This tablet explains their history, how a flash flood carved out the Grand Canyon, and wiped out most of them virtually overnight. We discovered the remains of one intact inside a cave on the Hopi Reservation my wife and I just visited.

"Note here." He pointed with a pen at the tablet. "It tells of the Navajo and Hopi Tribes that valiantly fought these ten-foot-tall giants, and incredibly, shows a model in a drawing. It's of the Earth."

Zooming in closer, the camera showed detail of the ancient drawing.

"This illustration shows a Flat Earth covered by a firmament dome. Note the land masses in the middle areas and seas all around. Encircling the perimeter, is a tall wall." He traced the edge with the point of the pen.

"Decoding the meaning, the markings denote the wall is made of ice! They knew!"

The attendees all came to their feet, cheering and hollering. A thunderous applause erupted.

The gray-haired man who followed her dad had his work cut out for him. The older, slight fellow had a big voice though. "Just call me the Flat Earther of Faith!" he boomed.

"Compare the conspiracies to understand the magnitude of this deception. They remove the gold standard and turn the government into a corporation. They take over the banking systems and governments through the illegal Federal Reserve System.

"They take out the leaders speaking of peace—John and Bobby Kennedy, Martin Luther King to name a few—to continue their war plans and silence those opposing their agenda.

"Kennedy wanted to stop the war in Vietnam before it got started. He wanted to return to the gold standard. Compare these conspiracies. Right here in Dallas you can take a tour of the grassy knoll where this great president was murdered.

"And now they corrupt the DNA of man with their unproven, mandated shots. Those remaining in God's holy image are under dire attack by the patent holders who claim to own any person—considered now to be a hybrid—who took their poisonous injections.

"It's all a cover up. They don't want you to know about the giants that once roamed the earth. Or that they're involved with organizations like CERN to return the Nephilim of old.

"Where can you find the answers for these supposed conspiracies, now coming to their fruition? Go to the Scripture! In the Bible, every answer to every question may be found. God's Word gives the ultimate solution.

"Our Creator sent a Savior. His name is Jesus. The times and the seasons say that He's returning soon! 'Prepare ye the way of the Lord,' John the Baptist commanded.

"And now it is up to those who believe in this truth, to prepare for the return of a Savior. This time, He comes not as a Lamb. This time, He returns as a Lion!

"This time, it says in Revelation, the Apocalypse, Jesus will return from heaven on the clouds, and the devil will be defeated and bound in chains. Then along with his fallen angels and demons, they will be thrown into the pit! That's Hades, or Hell. It's located below the Flat Earth.

"And then—there will finally be an everlasting peace on a beautiful stationary earth." As he wrapped up, many listening seemed dazed by the powerful words.

Slowly, the light applause turned into a chorus of Amens. The first from one little girl. Then another young man cried out, "Hallelujah!"

Later, one of the event organizers wondered out loud who invited the old man to speak.

"God invited him." A diminutive older woman answered who was standing nearby. "I would know because I'm married to the man."

Chapter Twelve

"He set the earth on its foundations so it should never be moved."   Psalm 104:5

With the gentle slapping of the ocean against his sailboat, Sam Benton wrote in his journal that morning as all the others. His grandson's note had opened his eyes along with his heart.

Nathan's plea rolled over again and again in his mind . . . 'I implore you, Grandpa, to consider faith once again.'

That the idea carried a certain appeal, he could not deny. Also, his grandson's appeal to consider God's true creation. He looked out over the water reflecting the sun with a million diamonds twinkling on its surface.

So beautiful.

Sam recalled meeting an old Naval Commander on a stopover in Fiji. The man had also given him several books including a Flat Earth Wiki report to study. He had learned much from the book his grandson gifted him, *Sailing Around the World Alone.*

He and Nathan would get along well on any voyage.

The beauty of God's creation *was* all around him whether calm or tempest. But always, the sea surrounded him. Water sought its own level—sea level.

In Cape Town, Sam met another old mariner from New Zealand, sitting on a porch swing at a weathered bait and tackle shop. Perched precariously on a rock that extended over several smaller seafaring boats, it afforded an excellent view of the harbor.

How could he know the brief encounter would change his perspective and turn his world upside down?

"Be ye English then?" The large older man puffed on a corncob pipe. "At my age, I know 'em well." He smiled a toothless grin.

"American. From the States, but you have a good eye. I had an English mother."

"I knew it. Ha! Seen it in ye eyes. The eyes don't lie." The man lifted a rattan hat to get a closer look, sizing Sam up. Fine by him since it gave him the perfect opportunity to do the same. He sized him up right back.

The old codger had to be ninety if he was a day! He wouldn't be surprised to discover he was a hundred.

"That's me boat there." He nodded towards a large schooner. "*The Sea Jenny,* I used to handle her myself, but the old gal gets away from me now. Have a fella name o' Skip. That be he there, tuggin' on the lines."

Surprised the man still sailed at his age, he grinned. "Beautiful craft, your *Jenny.*"

Swapping a brief exchange on their respective vessels, Sam consented to the old man leading him along a philosophical path.

"Let me ask you, friend, do ye know where ye are?"

"Think so—outside Madagascar, right?"

"I'm talking about the earth—about the seas. It's all around yet no one knows."

"What's the riddle then?"

The old salt smacked his lips. "Ye know, when I was a young whippersnapper, they taught it in school." The seasoned sailor obviously enjoyed dancing around the subject while luring in his prey.

"Give me a hint."

The man lifted an index finger into the air, sweeping the sky in a large circular motion. Then moving his arm straight towards Sam, his fingers extended one-at-a-time, palm down—as the arm moved back and forth slowly; steady.

Sam paused before shaking his head.

Finally, the old man spilled the whole barrel. "Ye ain't on no spinnin' earth man!" He waited, leaning in and staring into Sam's eyes. "Ye must know it from the seas, don'chee?"

Ah, just as he thought. Truth was, he had noticed much while sailing that conflicted with the globe model theory as Nathan touted.

"My grandson is writing a book on the subject. He believes in a Flat Earth."

"Sounds like a smart kid there." The old man reached for a hand-carved cane, grabbed it, and stood. "Follow me to the '*Jenny.*' I got somethin' for ye."

Slowly the man creaked along the dock, surprisingly steady though it rocked. The schooner had a smell of brine. "Don't drink anymore, or I'd offer ye a nip. Figure quittin's most likely the reason I'm still livin'…"

What a boon to be aboard the authentic schooner. 'Over a million miles at sea' one plaque read.

"Hey, Skip—grab me journal from the hold, will ye, Son?"

"Sure, Captain."

A few minutes passed while Sam studied the charts, but the young man returned with a large old binder. Retrieving it gingerly, the old seaman passed it over to Sam with an admonition:

"Listen, I been told I write better'n I talk. The old schools from Christ Church, down in Zealand gets credit for it. It's fer ye grandson. Give it to 'im. It's my proofs the earth is flat; me own writings and observations from over seventy years at sea, ye se."

"Oh, that is so generous. Are you sure about this?"

"Course I am! Twas a time skippers navigated without all those con-fangled gadgets."

Without waiting, the old man turned away. "Heading to bed, Sonny. Maybe see you up top afore we shove off in the morning."

"Thank you, sir. My grandson will highly value this for sure. Thank you." The old man disappeared, and Sam eased along the long plank back to the dock. Turning, he waved back at Skip, overwhelmed at the gift he'd received.

Pointing back at the binder Skip called out: "It's been his treasure, man. You must of really touched the old man's heart. Don't lose it or do anything stupid like trying to give it back."

"Wouldn't think of it." Sam hollered.

In the privacy of his berth, Sam carefully opened the old leather binder. From the beginning, the sailors' writings on God's stationary creation unfolded from a scientific perspective.

Earth is not a Globe – Proof 1.
"When I stand on the sands of the seashore and
watch a ship approach, I shall find that she will
rise to the extent of her own height, nothing more.

If we stand upon an eminence, the same law operates still, and it is but the law of perspective which causes objects, as they approach, to appear to increase in size until we see them right in front of us, the size they are in fact.

That there is no other rise than the one spoken of is plain from the fact that no matter how high we ascend above the level of the sea, the horizon rises on—and still on as we rise—so that it is always on a level with the eye though it be two hundred miles away as seen by Mr. J. Glaisher, of England, from Mr. Coxwell's balloon.

So a ship five miles away may be imagined to be 'coming up' the imaginary downward curve of the Earth's surface. But! If we merely ascend a hill such as Federal Hill, Baltimore, we may see twenty-five miles away on a level with the eye. That is, over twenty miles level distance beyond the ship that we vainly imagined to be rounding the curve and 'coming up!'

This is a plain proof that the Earth is not a globe.

It was at that moment, Sam realized he hadn't discovered the old man's name, but Nathan would love the divine gift. He trusted his grandson would one day share the journal with the world.

Perhaps even reaching those science-minded, making believers of them. Between Nathan and the journal, no doubt many would come to know God's true creation one day.

The Jenny's place at the dock had been left empty the next morning when Sam went to see if the old man was the Mister Glaisher mentioned who rode in the balloon. Guess he'd never know for sure.

Back at sea, Sam began transcribing the old journal. He didn't want for Nathan to have to wait for his return, plus, if anything crazy happened . . . the prize would be saved.

He'd send it by email to the boy on a stopover then present him the original threadbare journal after circumnavigating the earth. The official title told the tale. *100 Proofs that the Earth is not a Globe.*

He read another page from the old salt, that verified his own observations.

> Even a child knows that the angled crepuscular rays of the sun are not from millions of miles away as taught in school. They angle downward in a triangular pattern, impossible from vast distances.

Sam noted one personal observation of the sun at the end of each fair-weather day. At dusk, the sun always moved away from his perspective, gradually diminishing in size.

Never setting straight down, but always at an angle off into the distance.

Just like the Bible says, it's on a circuit. There is no such thing as a sunset. It wasn't a sundown either Sam knew for certain one night, as the sails flapped loosely in a light breeze.

The burning globe God hung in the sky to light His earth rode a circuit. Sam smiled, gazing heavenward. The clouds made him think of angels dancing in an azure sky.

On an island off Indonesia, he sailed in for supplies and met a missionary gal from the Azore Islands, and she impressed him in every way. The last day though, when he was about to leave, she tested him.

"The man I marry will know what it means to be 'equally yoked." At the time, Sam thought of the chickens' eggs' yolks, though he knew full well she spoke of walking together with God, being on the same path.

At dockside, she handed him an older King James Bible and bid him a Bon Voyage. "I'll be praying for the truth of this Holy Book to hit you in your heart, Sam Benton, and that you will come to know what real love means." Her eyes gazed upwards.

How long had it been since he encountered the language of believers outside his own family? Equally yoked . . . oxen were yoked together. Where one went the other had to go.

Her last words whispered into his ear as she hugged him carried a hint of hope. "I will pray that someday you will sail back into my life—filled with faith."

Rounding Chile, after tacking through a channel, Sam again made to shore for provisions and met another old Navy sailor assigned to the Antarctic for many years. Everything the salty seaman shared seemed to confirm what he'd been reading in the journal and Scriptures.

Something inside sensed it being a turning point . . . an opening of his eyes to the truth of the firmament and the shape of God's earth.

At night below deck, he often felt a deep glow in his heart, reading the Bible, or digesting the sea-faring strangers journal by candlelight. Russ sand Sue would be so surprised to find out how he spent the lonely evenings on his sailboat.

He chuckled to himself. Small swells lapped at the side of the ketch, while clanging bell-like sounds from lanyards and metal pulleys hitting atop the sails chimed in harmony with the splashing.

Each evening, he longingly transcribed a few more pages from the old man's lifetime of writings. There was one verse Sam found hard to decipher. He figured the old dog put it in there to confirm Flat Earth was in the original Bible.

And Urias sayd vnto Dauid: 'The Arck and Israel & Iuda dwell in pauilions: & my Lord Ioab and the seruauntes of my Lorde Iye in tentes vpon the 'Flatte Earthe'..."

II Samuel 11:11

Miles away on the West Coast, Dr. Thompsen texted Nathan. Undeterred by his firing, he'd found work as a lecturer at other faith-based universities. His talks led to a paid project on a Level Earth documentary.

The funds for the film came from a wealthy source who requested anonymity. The man suggested hiring assistants. Nathan would be a top choice if he had the time to commit.

Dr. Thompsen reached out in a message:

Listen, I'm working on a film with the current Title: Circle – Not a Ball. Two of my grad-students canceled on the project, and I could really use your help. It's a paid position but nothing to brag about. Interested?

***

Yes! Tell me when and where! Pay not that important. "I'm free!" The Semester ended yesterday.

Nathan typed, responding immediately. He'd heard something about the professor's film being made for a Netflix Documentary, approaching the subject from a perspective of facts and faith.

While working on the film, Nathan poured in many Scriptures with the narration.

"In Genesis 1:6, *"And God said, Let there be a firmament in the midst of the waters, and let it divide the waters from the waters."* And on the third day God made two great lights. *And God set them "In" the firmament of heaven to give light unto the earth;* the Sun and the Moon.

"It's a solid expanse; a tent sweeping over us. The Circuit of the Sun and Moon are in the dome and the whole thing rotates around the flat stationary Earth set on a foundation.

"That's why all the stars move around the sky as one set piece. That's why we see the same constellations in the same set locations, as people witnessed nightly, thousands of years ago. A solid blue ice dome separating the waters above from the seas below." He paused on *the seas below*, thinking of Grandpa. *Dear Lord, show him safe level seas.*

Eric Alan Soldal

Chapter Thirteen

"It is as high as heaven, what can't thou do? Deeper than hell, what can't thou know?"   Job 11:8

Riding along in the RV, Russ and Sue headed north out of Texas after the wonderful visit with their children. He had carefully wrapped the Cuneiform Tablet with blankets in a special pouch Chief de Chelly gave him.

Using Waze, they would traverse the safest back roads through the heartland of America to their new destination.

Russ had contacted a professor of ancient artifacts at Haverford University, in Pennsylvania, for further study of the Anunnaki Tablet. Along the way, he would decipher and translate what more he could from the ancient writings.

A road sign read, Entering Kansas.

Three hours later, Sue finally spoke over the hybrid engine humming along in the RV. "Kansas is so flat!"

"Interesting how we're noticing so much more of those sort of things now, isn't it?"

"But of course! We're really starting to understand we live on a plane and not a planet. It's harder to grasp hold of the truth when we've been taught all our lives that—"

"Tell me about it. I didn't want to believe. I thought Nathan was just trying his wings, being independent, but he was really on to something."

"That we live on a level plane will take some getting used to. Hey, do you think maybe that's why they call the flying machines airplanes?"

"Interesting thought." He chuckled. "Because pilots surely know better than most the Earth is a level plane."

"Or maybe that's why this land we're driving through now is a part of what's called The Great Plains." She played along, patting his shoulder.

"Right!" Russ grinned. "Our son texted a new joke this morning. How does a freemason Astro-n-o-t"—He spelled out the 'not' for his wife's sake—"change a lightbulb?"

"I have no idea. How?"

"They hold up the lightbulb, and the whole universe just spins around them!"

Sue's groan quickly became a smile. "Our boy."

A moment later, the RV's dash video screen lit up. Another warning from Ramos beginning with his source on a completely different topic.

The Coming Alien Deception, from my contact with Military Intelligence:

"It's about time for lunch anyway, what say we take a break and read this together? Then we'll be able to decipher it better."

"Sounds like a plan."

He crossed over a river and spotted a nice little roadside park, a perfect place for a well-deserved rest. While Sue prepared a light brunch, Russ hesitantly read the entire *Alien Deception Report* aloud.

The Pentagon has been engaging in another false narrative, claiming they have recovered a number of extraterrestrials and their crafts.

This has all been put in place so the population will fall for the great deception coming to this world, but here's my perspective on the UFO/Alien deception.

The Flat Earth truth is that we are not some random spinning ball, flying through space with other such balls. There are no planets—only wandering stars.

There is no other extraterrestrial life out there either. The only other ET life that exists are the fallen ones, The third of Heaven's angels who chose to follow Lucifer.

Those demonic entities have given way to disembodied spirits from the giants of old. CERN and the like are facilities where they are in communication with these evil beings.

Demons take many shapes and forms, but all are agents of the devil. Don't fall for the lies of NASA and the mainstream science community.

Those who are hellbent on a trans-humanism agenda, changing mankind's God given DNA.

Their big bang theory of the universe, giving us their evolution lie, has been fostered for thousands of years with the one goal being achieving their evil agendas.

We are now at the point where most will fall for the UFO Aliens agenda. It will lead to the enslavement of humanity.

The Bible warns us. God's Word guides His children to the Truth—the final authority for all things.

Once we come to that precious saving knowledge of Christ, we first submit ourselves to God, resist the devi, then he will flee.

Let us reborn of the light stay true to the Creator. We must keep our bodies—made in the very image of God—free from the devil's serums and the mark of the anti-Christ.

Share this only with those whom you trust.

In His Mighty Arms and Army, Brother Ramos

At the Newsroom in Manhattan, Gwen got a call from a climate watchdog, an emeritus, professor of geophysics, Guse Burkhardt. Her boss directed it to her after the previous night's *Cover Up Report* exposing the fake Global Warming climate agenda.

"Listen, Miss Sharpe, I'm with the Global Climate Intelligence Group., and I've just attended the conference in Belgium. Believe me, there is no climate emergency. The alarmist messaging being pushed by the global elites . . . It's purely political."

Gwen sat back in her chair. "Mister Burkhardt, may I assume you know of the World Climate Declaration document?"

"Yes, of course."

"Is it true that thousands of scientists and informed professionals have signed the document exposing the lies?"

"Absolutely. I've signed it. Our declaration states that climate science should be less political and climate policies more scientific."

"Sir, would you be available for an interview this evening for my *Cover Up Report*?

"I am, Miss Sharpe. I was hoping you might ask."

On air that night, she interviewed the man and two other scientists who signed the declaration. She asked Guse to explain the organization's objective.

"We are here to generate better knowledge with understanding for the true causes and effects of climate change as well as the effects of climate policy on our earth."

Gwen took a sip of coffee. "So, the declaration's signatories, besides yourselves, include Nobel laureates, theoretical physicists, meteorologists, professors, and environmental scientists worldwide. Is that correct?"

"Yes, ma'am."

"That's quite impressive." She shifted her weight, deciding exactly how to best phrase her next question. "Sir, can you please tell our viewers why you all signed a declaration that states outright that the so-called climate emergency is a farce."

The physicist to Professor Burkhardt's right spoke up. "I can tell you why I signed it. Because it's true."

"I signed the declaration because I believe the climate is no longer studied scientifically." Haym Benaroya, a distinguished professor of mechanical and aerospace engineering at Rutgers University added.

"The earth has warmed only two degrees Fahrenheit since the end of the Little Ice Age that occurred around 1850, but that hardly constitutes an emergency—or even a crisis— since the planet has been warmer yet over the last few millennia."

The men took turns telling the tale with hardly any prompting.

"There is evidence that average temperatures were higher during the so-called 'Medieval Warm Period' around the year 1000. During the 'Roman Warm Period', grapes and citrus fruits were grown in the now colder Britain, and in the 'Early Holocene Period' after the last regular Ice Age ended."

Nobel Prize laureate John Clauser was in the spotlight for challenging prevailing climate models, which he said ignored key variables, such as the clouds.

"I'd worked at some excellent institutions—Caltech, Columbia, and Cal Berkeley to name a few—where very precise science should be of the utmost importance. Reading the reports, I was appalled at the sloppiness of the work. Simply bad science."

"Many theories of anthropogenic climate change naturally focus on the effects of human-produced CO_2." Clauser sat forward, seemingly excited to get in his two cents.

"But these models overlook the significance of cloud dynamics." Referring to Al Gore's film, *An Inconvenient Truth*, the Nobel Prize winner added, "It's a totally artificial earth. The IPCC and others use artificial evidence. The cloud cover fraction fluctuates quite dramatically on daily and weekly timescales. We call this weather."

Gwen lifted up a stack of papers. "But they're the ones modifying and ruining the weather, right? According to this *Geo Engineering Watch* report, the governments are the ones destroying the earth with their chem trails and dusting the clouds with metals."

"This is correct, Miss Sharpe. They manipulate the weather in the name of saving planet earth It's a destructive, false science."

"But why do they do it? Is it for the money? Or are they trying to crash ecology for control?" Humph. Gwen paused. Didn't any of these noted scientists know about the true earth shape? That the Climate Czars fully intended to fill the dome with toxins . . .that they are spraying people like pests!

Before she could address the panel further, Dr. Clauser observed that human-induced climate change was shaping political agendas and influencing the strategic direction of entire nations.

"The whole world is doing it. A lot of the pressure comes from Europe. There's no need for all of these various world conferences."

With a cue from her director, Gwen summed up the information before her time was up.

"So in conclusion—correct me if I'm wrong—this so-called Climate Change is actually deceptive disinformation propagated and presented by various power-hungry politicians and rich men seeking to redesign and control the entire earth. The same ones who want to erase our Creator's true humanity. Wow!"

As the closing credits rolled, Alexander, the physicist, jumped in. "The climate emergency is fiction!"

As Sam maneuvered *The Juggernaut* next to the dock in Patagonia's port, a burly sailor hopped from his skiff, and assisted tying him off.

"Thank you, kindly, mate. Will you let me buy your dinner?"

"Not necessary, my friend, but I do love a good plate of swordfish." His gold-capped front teeth flashed when he smiled.

"Swordfish it is."

Turned out the man had been in the Navy assigned to an Antarctic Ice station. The conversation over dinner proved to be one of the most interesting and transforming tales about *The Blue Ice.*

"Supposedly, we were to take normal ice samples, but it was really all about *THE BLUE-SKY ICE.* That's what they called it." He spit out his air and shivered. "Three hundred degrees below sub-zero, I'm telling you. It never melts, just evaporates into thin air. And strong? We drilled through it over two miles at the edge of the earth.

"But a year later, our hole closed up on its own."

"Where was it? The ice?"

"All around the Queen Fabiola Mountains, a fifty-kilometer range slowing the glacial movement. It pushes the ice to the surface in places. It's the most beautiful color, an azure blue like nobody's ever seen.

"Swirling, textured turquoise surrounded the peaks and snow that remained during the Antarctic summer. The scientists said it connected from the edge of earth right over head and covered the sky."

"Amazing."

"You said it. The most beautiful sight imaginable. Thinking of it still thrills me to this day. Sometimes at night when I close my eyes and remember the journey, I'm at a corner of the earth once again, discovering the blue ice wall."

Before bidding the burly sailor adieu, Sam found himself caught up in the passion of the man's story and unexpectedly shared his own testimony—his service as a Naval Chaplin, the loss of his daughter, turning away from God, following the lure of money and power of Wall Street . . .

Then losing his dear wife who had remained resilient in love and faith throughout those years. He ended with how his solo voyage had rekindled an ember of trusting in God, how he believed the Lord was working on him.

"Need no convincing there, mate." The robust man lit up. "Jesus came walking to me on the ocean thirty years ago!"

As Sam pushed out to sea the next morning at as the sun lit the sky for the final leg of his epic adventure, he stood out on the deck, leaning against the wheel.

"Thank You, for enduring with me, Lord."

A powerful gust of wind filled the sails . . .almost as if in response.

Sea breezes and *The Juggernaut* had certainly taken him on the journey of a lifetime. His course in circumnavigation was by the Tradewinds. He had avoided the piracy routes of the Caribbean and Suez Canal, opting for a southern route to the Galapagos and then over the Pacific to French Polynesia.

From there, Sam island-hopped with a wary eye on the weather. That first summer, he had lit out for New Zealand through the Torres Strait, beating out two cyclones, then a stop in Northwest Australia and on to Indonesia took him into the Indian Ocean.

Most *around the world* sailors barrel through after that on one long passage, but Sam enjoyed the Maldives, Diego Garcia, and the Seychelle Islands for the winter. After, he beat it to South Africa, avoiding more pirates around the Horn.

Madagascar was like another planet--if there were such a thing as planets. He chuckled to himself, recounting his time at sea.

After rounding the Cape of Good Hope, it excited him to be back in the Atlantic and heading for home. A Northwest wind blew up as he hoped to make the Ascension Islands.

It had been over a year at the sails.

Late into the night a tempest raged and tossed *the Juggernaut* in the swells of the ocean. He found solace below deck, reading from the old 1611 Bible, another gift of God.

First, the old man's diary back in port at Cape Town, the Bible from the sweet Missionary gal and now this treasure from the Navy Engineer.

Finally, thankful to find harbor so close to shore without breaking apart on the reef, he dropped anchor. A line from an old hymn played over and over in his mind. 'In every high and stormy gale, my anchor holds within the veil.'

He trusted the Lord would hold him fast through the storm. Within, he experienced a sudden renewal. A feeling of hope with the deep faith that once gripped his heart rushed over him.

Waves crashing over the bow drenched him in a new baptism. Smiling skyward into the dark night, he prayed fervently for the first time in many years.

"Father in Heaven, thank you for remembering me. For restoring this lost lamb who loves You."

As Sam cradled in his berth below, he reached for the sealed package—the old 1611 Bible—and began reading by the light of an old gas lantern. He noted how carefully the Naval Veteran had inscribed pages, circled Scriptures and offered notes of support in the margins.

The book had been well cared for. The verses his eyes landed on pertained to a geo-stationary earth: *"Let there be a firmament."* Yahweh said.

"And Elohim said, let there be a firmament in the midst of the waters and let it divide the waters from the waters. And Elohim made the firmament, and divided the waters which were under the firmament from the waters which were above the firmament: and it was so." Genesis 1:6-7

Sam remembered in the day of Noah, when Genesis said, *'the fountains of the deep were broken up.'*

And in Genesis 8:2 it reported what happened after the flood. *"The fountains also of the deep and the windows of heaven were stopped, and the rain coming down from heaven was restrained."*

So, the water was above and below the earth. Heaven being above the firmament. He read on in Genesis about the firmament.

"And Elohim said, let there be lights in the firmament of the heaven to divide the day from the night; and let them be for signs and seasons, and for days, and years: and let them be for lights IN the firmament of the heaven to give light upon the earth: and it was so.

And Elohim made two great lights; the greater light to rule the day (the Sun) and the lesser light to rule the night (the Moon). He made the stars also.

And Elohim set them IN the firmament of heaven to give light upon the earth, And to rule over the day and over the night, and to divide the light from the darkness: and Elohim saw that it was good." Genesis 1:14-18

There was another revealing verse about the Sun. *"Its rising is from one end of heaven, and its circuit unto the ends of it."* Psalms 19:6

Sam paused considering the word *circuit*.

He wrote in the margins.

> Wow! It's a solid expanse; a tent sweeping over us. The Circuits of the sun and moon must be within the dome, and the whole thing —the whole thing meaning the dome and the sun and moon's circuits—rotates around a flat stationary earth. Stars move around the sky as one set piece.

He himself had witnessed the same constellations in the same set locations just as others witnessed nightly thousands of years ago. A solid blue ice dome separated the waters above from the great deep below.

He had found numerous verses where the sun is moving, but nowhere, not one place he'd come across, said the Earth moves around the Sun. On the last page, there was an old sketch of creation from a frontal view. It made Sam wonder about the Volcanos.

Maybe all that fiery, molten lava just bubbled up from the pits of Hell—or Hades.

Could it be the fire and brimstone mentioned in Scripture?

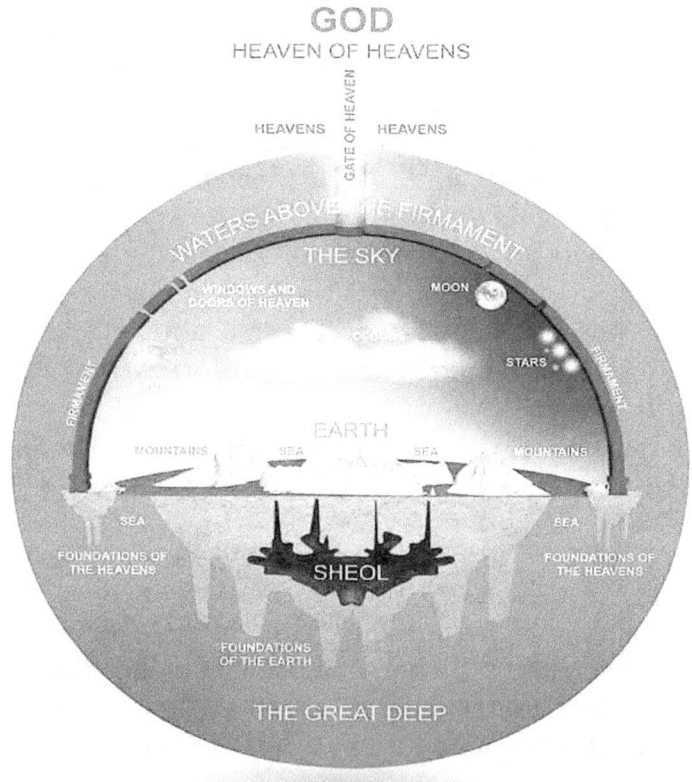

Chapter Fourteen

"The Lord gives the sun for a light by day and the ordinances of the moon and stars for a light by night."
Jeremiah 31:35

After the Cover-Up Report, Gwen waited in her small office at the station with the receiver to her ear for the call to be connected. Only the janitors were still working.

The man had instructed her to use only a landline, not to talk over a cell phone. After waiting for what seemed like hours, the call from her dad's old friend, Ambassador Ramos, finally came through.

"Gwen, hello! Hey, listen. Even though it isn't digital, it's better not to reveal too much over any call. Are you free to meet?"

"Yes, just let me know the time and place. I'll round up my cameraman and be there."

"Sorry, no cameras, dear. I'm sending via Telegram right now. Delete the message as soon as you retrieve the information, and make sure you remove your cell phone battery before you leave the city."

"How will I know you?"

"I'll be wearing an overcoat and holding a white cane. See you soon."

Notification came just as he'd said. She'd drive to Martha's Vineyard that very night to meet with him. It could be a huge story for her *Cover-Up Report*. She packed quickly, preparing to stay the night.

Was it about the ex-president involvement with the chef who died mysteriously there on the island?

While driving in the mist to the ferry, Gwen remembered the words her dad often used while comforting her as a child.

"We're a tough breed with thick skins, Daughter. The Bentons are a family that doesn't scare easily."

Whenever people tried to intimidate her, she remained strong in her convictions. Her mom would often add to the equation how bullies were often very wounded as a child.

But had revealing the truth threatened her very life?

For the first time in a long while, fear descended on her like a dark cloud. Recalling a verse Grandma Tilly often used, she resisted the emotion, quoting it aloud.

"For God does not give a spirit of fear, but one of power, love, and sound mind."

She longed to call Brad for comfort, but as instructed, she'd disabled her phone.

Another verse popped into her head *"I can do all things through Christ, who strengthens me."*

The two-hour drive from Manhattan seemed a blur of thoughts and lights. Flashing orange and yellow ones directed her to the shoreline where a hunk of rusting metal waited in the ocean, the ferry. A man in a yellow slickers waved a flashlight at her.

Gwen had specific instructions to meet the whistleblower in Martha's Vineyard at a seaside retreat called The Crucible. The name sounded ominously appropriate. Was she heading from the frying pan into the fire?

The ones set worldwide by the DEWS, the Defense Energy Weapons, crossed her mind. Even now the Texas oil fields and Cattle Ranchers were ablaze. Over a million acres burning overnight. Her own parents had assured her the man was one of the good guys. Once a military intelligence officer who had seen the light and wanted to expose the evil plans from the highest levels of power.

Gazing out into the dark waters beyond the ferry, she whispered a little prayer. her first in a while. "Dear Lord, please be with me through all of this. Keep Your angels of protection close by."

After a rocky thirty-minute ride over the choppy sea, a bullhorn bellowed from loudspeakers. Ferry workers came to life, casting lines to those onshore. With loud clanking sounds, a large metal door opened creating a ramp.

Patches of dense fog hindered the drive, but in only minutes, a sign appeared through the mist: The Crucible. Thank God, she made it. How long had she been holding her breath?

Hopping out, she went inside and scanned the lobby for a man wearing an overcoat holding a white cane. A man about her dad's age with dappled grey hair fit the bill.

"Mister Ramos?"

After a cordial greeting, he led her out onto a glass-enclosed, empty patio deck. Pulling out her chair with his cane, he motioned for her to sit.

"I've been in touch with your parents quite a lot recently."

"Yes, sir. I've heard a bit about you over the years. You met at a faith conference, right?"

"Fifteen years ago. I came to know Jesus as my personal savior through your father's testimony. We've been wonderful friends since. Studying and sharing with them sharpened my growth in the Lord."

"Aww, that's touching. I'm so glad to finally meet you." She kept her questions cordial. "So, you were at the Pentagon before becoming an ambassador?"

"That's right. In the European theatre . . . NATO, an Envoy, and with MI. The Obama Administration cleaned house, got rid of the stalwart old guard at the Pentagon. Most of us were conservatives."

"Why weren't you fired outright?"

"I believe the Lord kept the door open. He wanted me to stay, be a voice of concern and help expose evil."

In no time, she fired some serious questions. "Are they the ones responsible for taking out Kubrick after he filmed a Masonic type of devil worship event in the film *Eyes Wide Shut*?"

"I believe so. He filmed much of it in one of the Rothchild's own mansions in Great Britain and patterned the scenes based on the family's own elite events at their Chateau outside of Paris."

"I've heard they cut twenty-six minutes out of the film. Do you know that to be true and why they did it?"

"They were deleted, yes. There were . . . well, let's just say that portion contained scenes with children. Farther along, satanic rituals alluding to necromancy, and even the drinking of blood."

"How awful!" What a horrifying thought. "The rich and powerful families really do those things?"

"Well, presently the big thing is adrenochrome. They frighten the children before—well, you know—before their . . . umm . . . demise."

"Oh, my Lord! Why?"

"Are you sure you want to know, Miss Benton?"

"Yes, I need to."

"It' used to excite or adrenalize the blood before they drink it, usually administered through a monoclonal procedure."

"Ouch—the sorcerers make it sound medicinal."

"Exactly. The other is done during their demonic rituals."

"So sad." Her vision blurred as tears filled her eyes.

"Are you alright, hearing all this?"

"I hate it, of course, but the truth needs to come out."

Oh Lord, she prayed silently. Help me hold it together. Somehow, this must be stopped.

The conversation continued exposing more of the evil agenda of the Freemasons, shocking her with each new revelation. How could men—and women—who have so much, be so wicked?

Freemasonry Oaths

The obligation of a first degree Freemason (Entered Apprentice degree):

"Binding myself under no less a penalty than that of having my throat cut across, my tongue torn out by its roots, and buried in the rough sands of the sea at low-water mark, where the tide ebbs and flows twice in twenty four hours, should I ever knowingly or willingly violate this my solemn oath and obligation as an Entered Apprentice Mason. So help me God, and keep me steadfast in the due performance of the same."

When she could stand no more, she switched topics.

"So, what difference, if any, do you believe it will make to the world knowing we live on a Level Earth and not a round spinning ball? May I tape this answer?"

The dapper man's face contorted then smoothed. "Go ahead."

"Thank you so much." She turned on her recorder.

"Deception becomes power. It isn't only the deception by NASA, but world powers. Russia, China, India, and Japan all have space programs now. And the lies go all the way to the top."

Ramos spoke passionately as he scanned the patio.

"It's more about the lie than it is about the shape of the earth, my dear. Controlling powers have perpetrated the heliocentric lie. They've created a facade designed to blind mankind and keep them in the dark about God's true creation."

"Like telling us we have descended from monkeys?"

"Exactly."

"But why the lie? Is it for the money?"

"Partly, but not completely. NASA costs taxpayers billions of dollars used for their covert operations. Those at the top don't need the money. They print the money. Bucketsful of paper and plastic credit cards, or they conjure it up out of thin air."

"Like Bit Coin, or the coming Central Digital Bank Currency?"

"They create money every second of every hour of every day. The trillion-dollar Rothschild family doesn't need more money."

Another of Grandma Tilly's old adages came to mind: *"The love of money is the root of all evil."* The greedy ones who never consider, *"They pierce themselves with sorrows."*

Her own parents reminded her of this and how money would often lead even those faithful people astray.

Something had to be done.

"Do they perpetuate the Masonic lie for power then?"

"Again partly, but not really . . . The world's ruling class families, like the Windsor's, routinely install the world's kings and leaders on evil earthly thrones, eliminating the ones who refuse to play their games."

"So what is it then? Control?"

"That's what it boils down to, yes. It is about control." Ramos took in a deep breath and breathed it out slowly. "It's a facade being brought that is not for our benefit. The magnitude of the deception . . . It's difficult to grasp. There are unwritten codes among the elite evil doers."

"It seems they almost brag about them, doesn't it?"

"The Illuminati and the Masons have a secret code to warn people of an evil deed they intend to perpetrate before it is implemented. It's in their unwritten by-laws. It goes to superstitious thinking; that if no warning is given, negative karma or bad repercussions will come upon them.

"Here's the caveat. They are hoping people in general will not notice or heed the warnings because they consider mere humans as stupid imbeciles. Basically, they believe only the elites deserve to live."

"That's right. A code of the wicked, and in the dark spiritual realm, the pride of Satan looms. Isn't it true that Lucifer, same as many earthly criminals, cannot contain his boasting?"

Gwen sighed, adjusting herself in the oversized armchair. It was late. She noticed the servers had left. "So, getting back to the fake moon landing. My brother says NASA is Masonic and that they lie about God's true creation."

"That's right."

"Why would they say we live on a globe and hide the true shape of the earth?"

"That answer goes to what happens when people are isolated into believing falsely that they are on a blue marble in a vast universe. It makes them insignificant. The lie that there are billions of other stars, other planets, and trillions of other worlds with a high probability of other civilizations—all the more insignificant.

"Like one ant in an anthill. They want you to believe that you evolved from a one cell organism and crawled out of the primordial soup to become a monkey and then a man.

"People who believe their myth have more faith in a lie than in wisdom. Scripture says, *'The fear of the Lord is the beginning of wisdom.'* The lie removes God from the equation.

"Is it a salvation issue, you may ask? It has been for many who stopped believing in a divine and Holy Creator. To them, it doesn't matter what the Bible says—so called 'science' corrects the Bible and introduces doubt, confusion, and lies."

"My brother also believes it is a salvation issue because so many folks and Flat Earthers who finally come to believe the true shape of the Earth also come to believe in Jesus."

"In a way, your brother is right. It is about salvation for those who come to faith after believing in God's fixed earth."

"It's just that not many are open to the truth." Gwen glanced out the tall windows. Battering rain ran down the glass, fracturing the lights in the darkness outside.

"It's easier to get them to believe they came about as some sort of accident. When people believe the round earth ball lie, their minds become more malleable to the idea that there is no God.

"They believe there is no Creator, and all of this we observe just came about by accident. And because of this great lie, it gives the controllers a platform to build other deceptions upon."

"So, money also becomes a deception tool?"

"Those demonstrative ones in control who print the money perpetuate the myth. Money only maintains the value that people ascribe to it. The devil uses it to keep humanity enslaved.

"People go to work for a pittance while the elite tax most of what they take home. They want people living paycheck to paycheck."

"So, it's a form of enslavement then?"

"It is. Mental, physical, spiritual—in every possible way, they seek to enslave mankind. If you are a faithful believer who knows the Lord, it becomes apparent this has been Satan's plan all along.

"Blinding humanity to believe we are insignificant and there is no Creator God . . . That we are on a speck traveling through a vast universe of time and space. Satan being the Prince of the Power of the Air has planned from the beginning to destroy mankind made in God's image."

"He doesn't want us knowing we are special and how greatly we are loved by our Creator."

"Precisely. People need to understand how important they are to God, how He created us to be in relationship with Him, and how they bring value to humanity, through having faith in the Lord God Almighty."

Gwen chimed in: "Yes! Scripture says we are beautifully and wonderfully made. That God knew us in our mother's womb, before we were even born." She took in a deep breath and smiled.

"So, you're saying awareness to the level of this deception will change things?"

"My hope is that when people wake up and realize we are at critical mass with 'wars and rumors of wars,' those with open eyes will band together. More brave soldiers in God's army, exposing the lies, those involved, and their fake institutions."

"It's so much."

"It is, but the globalist perpetrators have got to be exposed. Their agenda is preposterous!"

Ramos reached inside a leather case at his side and handed her a thick package. "Many years of research went into this intel. Use it with discretion. Several of my old colleagues believe the evil ruling elite have been at the seat of power for centuries."

"And you?"

"Ruling classes are real. Their code of silence the higher-level Illuminati and Masons must recite and keep under penalty of death is real." He paused momentarily staring at the candle, flickering on the table.

"Men's hearts are inherently wicked. Our only way out is through our Lord and Savior. I believe with all my heart that Jesus is returning for His true church. That's us, right?" He broke into a broad grin.

"Yes, sir. Definitely—that's us!"

"One more thing, Gwen…"

"Yes?"

"You may have guessed another reason I asked you to meet me at Martha's Vineyard. It has something to do with your story on the ex-president's chef, who was eliminated here. Found floating near the mansion in four feet of water."

"You mean killed?"

"Listen—the man was working on a tell-all book. There's a former secret-service agent who will meet you tomorrow morning in the lobby at eight o'clock."

"How will I recognize him?"

"Everything is outlined in the documents I just passed to you. That and a history of the elite's secret plans for humanity. Strictly off the record though."

"Will you be here?"

"Let's just say that I will be close by at all times."

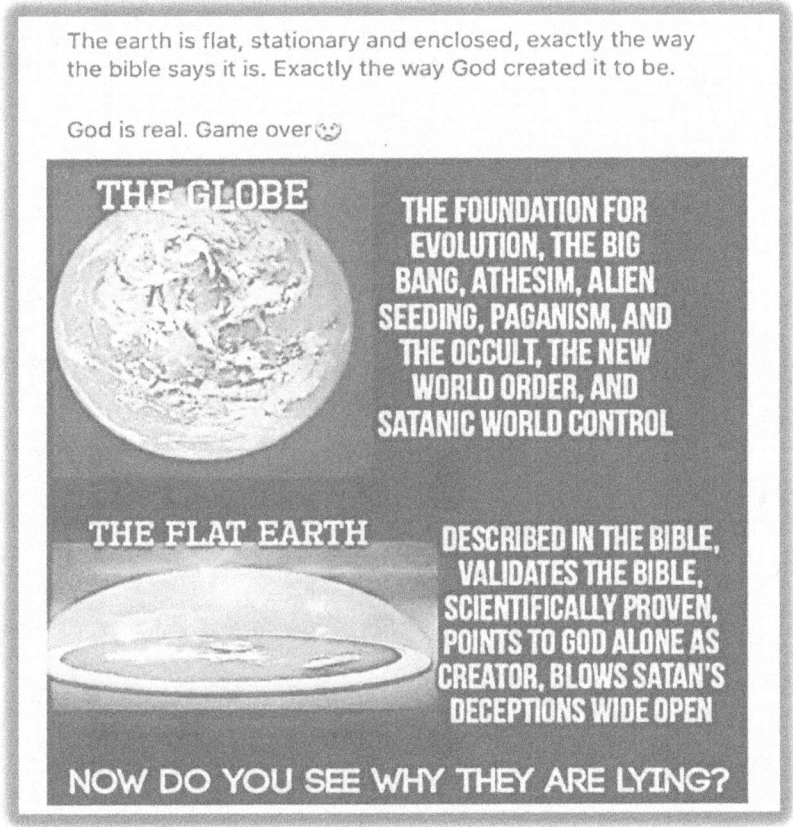

Chapter Fifteen

'The Lord gives the sun for a light by day and the ordinances of the moon and stars for a light by night.'
Jeremiah 31:35

Exhausted, Gwen pulled back the comforter at the Martha's Island Inn. Knowing it would be three hours earlier out west, she turned her phone on just to call her great-grandma in Pasadena. A caretaker answered saying she was already fast asleep.

Early to bed must be one of the reasons for the sweet lady's longevity. Her ninety-seven faithful years brought a smile. What a blessing Nathan could be living so close—one of the reasons he picked U.C.L.A.

Her brother mentioned stopping by to visit their great grandma on a regular basis.

Gwen turned her cell off and put in a wake-up call with the front desk, then crawled under the covers in her ocean-front room.

"Thank you, Lord, for this day, for Your love, protection, and truth. I love you, Jesus."

The new day lit the room, and she opened her eyes to a beautiful view. Stepping onto the second-story teak deck, she was met with a blast of sea spray and fresh air. The storm had passed.

Thoughts turned to her grandfather out on the ocean for the past several months. He would be rounding the Cape in South America soon if he hadn't already. Though she understood and admired his desire to be off grid, she sure missed talking with him.

Such a welcome distraction, gazing out at the vast waters and thinking about him on his fancy sailboat. She grinned, recalling her brother's words. 'Whenever you look out at the ocean, remember water always seeks its own level.'

"It's level, Nathan. It's flat!"

Determined to pray daily for Grandpa's safe return, she made a single cup of coffee and sat out on the deck to pray but found it hard to concentrate after spending most of her restless night going over the documents Ramos had passed to her—that and processing her interview with him.

What chilling information.

The report titles alone proved ominous enough with *The NASA War Document*, *The Silent Weapons Document*, or *The Iron Mountain Document*, from 1954, detailing the first Bildeburger's meeting, and the like.

It would be hard to get any of it past the network cronies. After she finished praying, she checked her watch and picked up the pace while dressing. Only fifteen minutes before she needed to be downstairs to meet the secret service agent.

On her way out the door, the phone on the nightstand rang with staccato bursts. *Shhring! Shhriing! Shraang!* She dropped her bag in the open doorway and ran to pick it up.

"Yes?"

Suddenly, two men burst into her room. One stood in the doorway while the other rushed toward her.

Gwen held out the receiver and yelled.

"Stop!" Surprisingly, the men halted in their tracks. Waiting...

Silence fell over the room and then a voice was heard on the other end of the phone. "Is this Gwen Sharpe?"

"It is."

"The former President of the United States is waiting for you downstairs."

Being escorted by the two big men in dark suits caused a sickening feeling to come over her. Jerking her arms free, they steered her without touching her on either side.

"I think I'm going to be sick. I best visit the lady's room."

One answered in a crass tone. "Maybe she's pregnant, or something."

She covered her mouth and made a retching sound. "I'm heading to the restroom, and you better not stop me."

Inside the black and white tiled bathroom, Gwen attempted to collect herself—adrenaline pumping. She leaned close to the mirror. "What are you going to do now, young lady?"

What could they do to her in public? Besides, surely the ex-agent would be out there for their meeting. Would the President or other agents recognize him? He wouldn't let them hurt her . . . and Ramos said he'd be watching . . .wait! An idea came to her in a flash. She reached inside her bag retrieving a small Go-Pro video camera.

She took her time, letting the two men wait. She would turn the tables. Then stepping back out with a wet towel to dab her face, concealing the camera, they escorted her toward the front doors where a fancy black SUV waited.

The graying ex-president stepped out.

"Thank you, gentlemen." He grabbed her hand roughly.

Gwen glared, pulling away. "I do not appreciate your tactics. You have no right to harass me like this."

In a blaze, Gwen reached down lifting her video camera right up into the ex-president's face, changing her tone.

"Thank you for meeting me here in Martha's Vineyard, Mr. President. You once said that the highest altitude any NASA craft could go was low earth orbit. Why?"

Caught off-guard, one of the agents reached cautiously for Gwen's arm and the filming camera.

Suddenly, another man walked up to them wearing a beret and dark glasses, lowering the agent's arm forcibly.

"Darling, you're late. If we don't leave now, we'll miss our flight."

Late. She was late. Was he the ex-agent? He had to be. The stranger took her arm, and she played along wrapping hers through his. He glanced toward the President. "You'll excuse us, sir."

A sense of calm came over her as he escorted her away.

When they were out of hearing range, he confessed. "I'm the former secret service agent you were to meet."

"I figured as much. Where are we going?"

"Ambassador Ramos arranged a car, and he's waiting to drive us to your office downtown."

"What about the president and his goons?"

"Don't worry about them. He wouldn't dare cause a scene in public. Plus, I heard your question. That will throw them!"

Back in the newsroom her boss appeared sympathetic for once. "You did the right thing getting out of there. This guy who rescued you—he's here?"

"Yes, sir. He has quite a story, and he's willing to go on the air tonight."

"You know, Gwen, there's no turning back after this."

"I know…but someone has to expose these people and their evil lies. Plus, I've got someone watching over me."

"That definitely seems to be the case." Roger grinned. "And he's bigger than any glorified security guard."

Hmm—could it be Roger had found a little faith?

"After all this though, I'm going to need a few days off. My brother and an ex-professor of his have collaborated on a film, and there's a premier in Virginia Beach. My entire family is coming back to the homestead for the weekend."

"What's the film about?"

"It's on the true Biblical shape of the earth."

Roger hung his head, slowly moving it side-to-side. "The head of the Network is still mad at me about airing your program and highlights from that conspiracy convention."

"I thought the ratings were good."

"Oh, we took all the top spots that week, probably the only reason we still have our jobs." Roger gave a nod towards the door. "No wonder you asked that crazy NASA question."

"Hey, it did distract them. If you're interested, you're welcome to attend. A beach getaway would be good for you!"

"We'll see. Looking forward to your program tonight, kiddo. Hoping this secret agent vicarates ex-President *O'Bummer*, that grimy politician—for that matter—all the snakes who believe they are above the law."

After the program aired, the station switchboard lit up for hours. Calls for a Senate investigation into all of the ex-Presidents' exploits—not only the death of his chef—were thrown out there from several directions.

The FBI and Department of Justice, presumed to be compromised and possibly complicit in the cover up, would be of no help. Thankfully, secret service agents had named names in the broadcast. Many opponents had been taken out.

Gwen's *Secret Agent Cover-Up Report,* as it came to be known, spread worldwide overnight. The material provided by Ambassador Ramos had been incremental for the expose.

The following morning, Roger shielded his number one reporter from several death threats.

"It's good you're getting out of town for a few days, Gwennie. Every reporter and crackpot in the world will be after you now . . . afraid you've become part of the story."

"I'm not afraid."

"That's right, I forgot. You have a heavenly host of protection, don't you?"

"Yes, sir!"

Another huge buzz ensued even before the *Circle Not a Globe* documentary premiered in theatres. Netflix bought the rights to the film planning to air the program Nationwide. Professor Thompsen and Nathan had even used Stanley Kubrick's fake moon landing footage along with his confession.

Nathan encouraged the professor's attentions to his sister. He'd love nothing more than the man being a brother, and his professor had admitted he planned a future out east to be closer to Gwen.

He enjoyed being included on a couple of outings with his sister and her new beau. What really made him smile, though, was when his cell rang, he looked down, and saw it was Myiah!

"Hey, you! What a great surprise! How have you been?"

"Me? Oh, I'm great! Blessed! I am at the airport here in Virginia Beach, Mr. Nathan."

"What? That's an even better surprise! Wow. I'll come pick you up!"

"No, no. I can take a cab and be there in the no-time. Then we have more time together! I'm so glad you're surprised! I didn't want to miss the show!"

That evening, before the documentary aired, Gwen received a call from her boss. "I know you're off, but I have an important assignment for you later this afternoon."

"Roger, you know we have a special showing of my brother's film, and the whole family is here, including our great-grandma. I don't have any extra time."

"Well, this won't take long, I promise. I'm having a camera man meet you on the docks at the marina there. You can't let me down here, Gwennie. Won't take but a minute. Can you be there at five? You know I wouldn't ask if it wasn't important."

"This isn't fair, and I don't like it one bit, but I guess I'll do it for you."

Waiting on the dock at five minutes after five, about ready to leave, she heard an old man holler.

"Ahoy there!"

The voice was familiar. Wait . . . She spun around. Grandpa sailed right up to the dock in The Juggernaut! How wonderful! He tacked it right into a birth to the buzz of a nationwide media standing onshore.

It would make quite a headline: *Wall Street man sails alone around the world with Surprise Return!* Roger was definitely right. She wouldn't have missed it for the world! Because of the media press, Gwen and her camera man had a hard time getting close. Her family waved from the dock.

The first rival reporter to meet Grandpa shoved a microphone into his face and asked what he had discovered. He answered with four words:

"Big Seas, Flat Earth!"

Pushing his way through the press, Sam reached her and lifted her off her feet in his strong arms. Again, she became part of a story televised worldwide, one that proved much brighter and happier. Sam almost glowed, basking in the love of his precious granddaughter. He wanted to surprise her.

"This is my granddaughter, Miss Gwen Sharpe, the famous investigative journalist! My grandson's film is premiering here tonight!"

"It's called *Circle, Not a Globe*," Gwen reported.

Chapter Sixteen

"When He established the heavens, I was there, When He inscribed a circle on the face of the deep..."
Proverbs 8:27

In the Old Grand Theatre downtown, Nathan and Professor Thompsen's documentary premier aired with all the Bentons in attendance. Nathan's parents, sister, Great-Grandma Tilly. Extras included the Ambassador Ramos, Uncle Tomas, Auntie Jan, and now even Myiah.

The media coverage astounded him. A lot of thanks in that arena probably belonged to his sister. It seemed the whole family supported him and *Level Earth* at that film festival in Virginia Beach.

In the lobby, Russ felt a tap on the shoulder. It was young David from the *Flat Out Earth – Flat Out Lies,* documentary they had befriended during the filming in Myrtle Beach.

"Hey! I'm here with my dad, mom, and sisters. It's so good to see you again!

"You too there, young man! How did your filming go?"

"If you're wondering, all those globe trotters are chicken!"

"What do you mean, globe trotters?" Russ shook the boy's hand vigorously.

"I mean nobody stepped up to challenge the surveyor, who offered the hundred thousand dollars to anyone who could prove him wrong, remember?"

"Sure we do." Sue stepped up to join them.

"There was no curve in sixty miles of beachfront. He's proved it all right. Flat as a pancake...through the lens we could see the hotel buildings over sixty miles away."

"We heard you could even see people walking on the beach." Sue smiled.

Abruptly, David turned and ran off towards a group of girls.

Sue stifled her own laugh, whispering to her husband. "Did you see he was dressed like Barney Fife from the old Andy Griffith Show?"

"What a great kid. Must be home schooled."

Nathan was excited to meet *The Founded Earth Brothers* from North Carolina, who were known for faithful documentaries of their own.

Before the evenings premier aired, Brother Josh opened the festivities giving a welcome and brief presentation on the big screen entitled: *Ancient Cosmology*. A well-researched historical guide to God's true earth model. After a resounding applause, the lights lowered.

Anticipation was high.

The documentary began with a film showing the Apollo astronauts walking around on a sound stage. A movie set.

All is silent as you see the cameramen, scaffolding, and fake moon surface and space backdrops. Neil Armstrong and Buzz Aldrin are bouncing around on the fake moon surface while hooked to wires.

Suddenly, a narrator broke the silence. "The entire Bible supports Geo Stationary Earth model. In Isaiah 44:24 the Creator says, *'I am the Lord, who made all things, who alone stretched out the heavens, who spread out the Earth myself.'*

"Speaking of the Firmament the Word says *'He bowed the heavens also.'* in 2nd Samuel 22:10. The Scripture says that all liars will have no part in the Kingdom of God."

A moment later the title appeared, *Circle NOT a Globe.*

"Stanley Kubrick confesses, 'I was involved in fraud. I was the film director of the fake moon landing.' A worried Kubrick added, 'The CIA-orchestrated footage was filmed in the desert outside of Hollywood.' "

After more NASA footage showing failure after failure, fake after fake, and a Space X craft shown skidding across the firmament above the earth.

"God made the Firmament Impenetrable," the narrator stated, and the film adeptly segued into the Creation.

"The sun, moon, and stars were created by God on the fourth day of creation and placed 'In the firmament' or inside of His atmosphere. The stars were also placed inside for times and seasons.

"It is a dome covering. The firmament bows. In the *Strong's Concordance*, the bow here refers to 'bend', being bended over. The Heaven bends around the Earth."

A blinding close up of the Sun filled the screen. Gwen, who was cozied up with Brad in the dark theatre, covered her eyes nestling her head into his shoulder. The deep voice of the narrator continued on.

"The Sun is a luminary. A light. Sixty-seven Bible references to the Sun moving, but nowhere, not one place—zilch, nada, zero—indicates the Earth moves around the Sun.

"The Bible says that the sun has a repeating circuit around the circle of the earth. Mainstream science purports that the universe is expanding continually with the earth spiraling outward from the Milky Way Galaxy at over 2.2 million miles per hour.

"The circuit of the sun varies. There are different circuits for different seasons of the year; the sun's daily path transitions in a spiral from one seasonal circuit to the other. It is on a loop that heats everything under the dome.

"If the earth were spherical, and the sun was millions of miles away, you would never be able to see the sun's long reflection on the sea at dusk. The rate of drop-off would not provide enough surface area because the sunlight would be angling away from your perspective.

"Reflections of the long sunlight are due to one reason only. The ocean is flat.

"Psalm 19:6 says: *'His going forth is from the end of the heaven, and his circuit unto the ends of it: and there is nothing hid from the heat thereof.'*

"That it is a light in the firmament to rule the day."

"And about the moon. . . A scripture appeared on the screen. *'And God made two great lights . . . and the lesser light [the moon] to rule the night.'* Genesis 1:16

"The moon *does not* reflect the sun's light as man's science would have you believe. It has its own light. As the sunlight is physically hot, the moon's light is physically cold. Jeremiah 31:35 says *Thus saith the LORD, which giveth the sun for a light by day, and the ordinances of the moon and of the stars for a light by night, which divideth the sea when the waves thereof roar; The LORD of hosts is his name:*

"The scripture is saying that 'The Lord gives the sun for a light by day and the ordinances of the moon and stars for a light by night.' The ordinances refer to their circuit.

Professor Brad appeared on the screen! The theatre erupted in applause. "They say the moon just reflects the sun's yellow light. But the moon is pale in color, even when seen during the daytime. They say the sun is a yellow color because of atmosphere.

"But the sun and moon are not the same color. Why? So why isn't the light from the moon the same color as the light from the sun, when it travels through the same atmosphere?

"The truth is they are both inside the same atmosphere—inside the firmament. The truth is that the moon has its own light. It is a light. Such as a plasma light to cool the night. And for signs and seasons.

"How can any spacecraft land on a light? They can't, because the moon is not a round rock. The Bible says the moon is, **'the lesser light to rule the night.'** Those who study the domed earth model believe that no spacecraft have ever landed on the Moon or Mars. All faked for political, monetary, control, or even spiritual reasons.

"With the tides, they are magnetic, not based upon gravitational pull. The sun giving a positive charge and the moon a repealing negative one."

"The Sun & Moon are local (close) with the same circumference, within the Firmament.

Suddenly, Nathan appeared on the screen in a darkened room. Several hoots and hollers rang out from family members. "What about a solar or lunar eclipse?" he said. "Everyone is eclipse crazy these days."

He held up a flashlight 🔦 as an example of the sun, and

a penny 🪙 as an example of the moon. Passing the coin slowly over the light, it was covered completely in the dark room.

The light being completely dark, created a corona effect around the edges. Slowly Nathan finished passing the penny over the flashlight and the effect was just like a solar eclipse! The full light was restored.

"The Sun & Moon, are on their own circuits, where God the creator established them like a clock; for times and seasons; so the moon is like a second hand and sun like the hour hand. During an Eclipse of the sun, the moon is lapping the sun, on the same circuit, covering its surface." Nathan explained.

"When you see them both in the sky at the same time and they're shielded by the clouds, you can visually see the sun and the moon are the same size. It's observable. It's common sense.

"Interesting, that it explains this in depth in The Book of Enoch. 'Sun & Moon have the same circumference. . .' "

At this point in the film premier, the entire Benton family and group of friends erupted in cheers for Nathan. Myiah, who was sitting with Nathan, leaned in and kissed him on the cheek!

Momentarily, large photos of a level earth appeared from 100,000 feet, taken from amateur weather balloons, the subtitles read. Then NASA photos appeared from the same height showing a false curve, taken from a convex lens.

The booming narrator continued. "There is no width or length on a ball."

"Job 11:8 tells us *'It is as high as heaven, what can't thou do? Deeper than hell, what can't thou know?'* and verse nine continues *'The measure thereof is longer than the earth, and broader than the sea.'*

"You can't have length or breadth, width, on a ball. The globalists and University communities have been creating flat earth maps they say are based on the globe 'for more accurate measurements.'

"Headlines read: 'Astrophysicists create the most accurate flat earth map ever.' Alexander Gleasons's 19th Century Flat Earth Map was the standard back in the day for navigation on the seas.

The noted 'physicist' Tyson, who has lost debates to flat earthers, says that the earth is now 'pear shaped.'

The Bible doesn't say circumference or ball globe. It's a flat earth on a flat level plane. It's flat.

Use wisdom with faith.

Do you believe that all of the Bible is true?"

"Colossians 2:8 says: *'Beware lest any man spoil you through philosophy and vain deceit after the traditions of men, after the rudiments of the world, and not after Christ.'*

"Would water ever stay on a spinning ball traveling at over a thousand miles per hour? Water always seeks its own level. That's why it is called 'water level.'

"The Bible makes it clear that a **Circle is not a Ball**." The narrator emphasized the documentary title. "The Prophet Isaiah uses different Hebrew words for each. 'Chug' means *'circle, vault, or horizon'* according to the Strong's Concordance. (2329), and the noun 'Bol' refers to ball. It translates as *'ball, sphere, a round pill, or globe.'*

"Since twirling a globe around in their first classroom, so many believers believe they are on a globe planet, spinning endlessly in space. That belief has become an epidemic.

"Many claim to believe in the Bible at the same time. Some even holding on to the false claims of modern science such as *The Big Bang Theory* and *Evolution vs Creation*.

"Even at The Ark Experience—the model of Noah's Ark—in Kentucky, they hire lecturers who portray a false theory. A spinning globe in space opposed to what the Bible says.

"But Isaiah knew the difference between a ball, a sphere, and a circle, and so did the KJV English Bible translators."

Several scriptures rolled along with the commentary:

"Proverbs 8:27 ***When he prepared the heavens, I was there: when he drew a circle upon the face of the depth:*** How do you inscribe or draw a ball into something? You can't. No. In each of these cases, we are talking about a circle.

Job 38:13-14 'That it might take hold of the ends of the earth, that the wicked might be shaken out of it? It [the Earth] is turned as clay to the seal; and they stand as a garment.'

"Where are the 'ends of the Earth' to take 'hold of' on a ball? This description fits perfectly with a circular Earth, which is pressed as a seal.

"Get some wax and a seal. Press the seal into the wax, and you will get the picture. You end up with a circular, pressed, flat seal with raised features on it. It is clue from God.

"And it says that in the end, the angels will gather all those believers in Jesus Christ, who have the Mark of God from 'the four corners of the earth.' You can't have corners on a ball. But by using geometry, one can circumference a circle, inscribing four points, or four corners. The Bible repeatedly refers to 'the ends of the earth.'"

The narrator segued into the power of understanding words. "Do not words have deep meanings." He echoed.

"He will surely violently turn and toss thee like a ball into a large country." Isaiah 22:18

"It is He that sitteth on the circle of the earth." Isaiah 40:22

"Isaiah knew the difference between a CIRCLE and a BALL. The KJV translators knew the difference. Do you know the difference?" The narrator challenged.

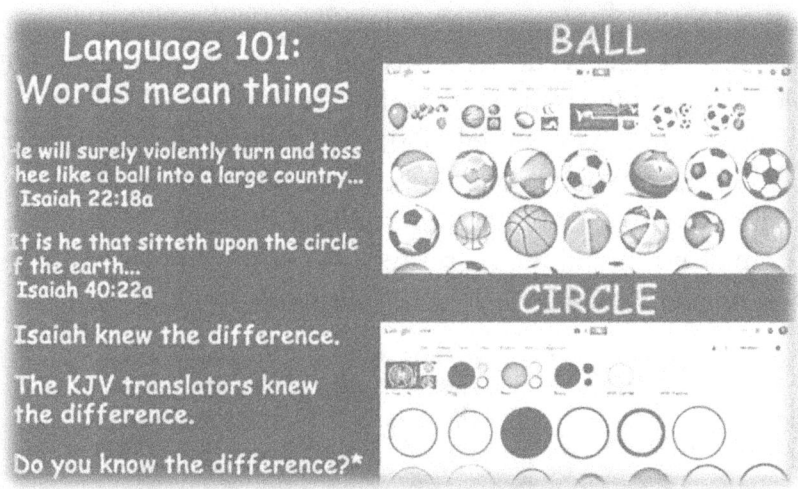

Wrapping up, Professor Brad and Nathan both appeared, taking turns sharing a message on the sun, moon and seasons, translated from the original Hebrew.

"There are twenty-two letters in the Hebrew alphabet, and it reads right to left. It's God's first language to His children."

"When a child in Israel is first learning verses, they place a bit of honey right on the scripture and have the child taste it! They want the child to make the connection that the word of God is sweet." Nathan smiled.

"And now we do it backwards. God's Word tells us to use the moon to tell time, and what do we do? We switch it around and science wants us to tell time by the sun."

"Our calendar is completely off from the times of God and his appointed feasts' schedules. It means nothing to most people because they've been blinded by the false sun god, Helios." The professor pointed to a large photo of the deity.

"But they are really being blinded by the devil." Nathan added. "The word 'Heliocentric' came from this pagan sun god, Helios. Faith in heliocentrism is a superseded astronomical model where the earth and so-called planets revolve around the sun at the center."

"Don't be deceived. We're living on a level plane and not a planet. You are significant to the Creator!" Brad finished.

The large screen suddenly flashed spectacular photos of the level earth. Sounds of angelic harps and orchestral strings resonated loudly, as the credits rolled.

Free promotional movie posters were offered in the theatre lobby as people were leaving the showing.

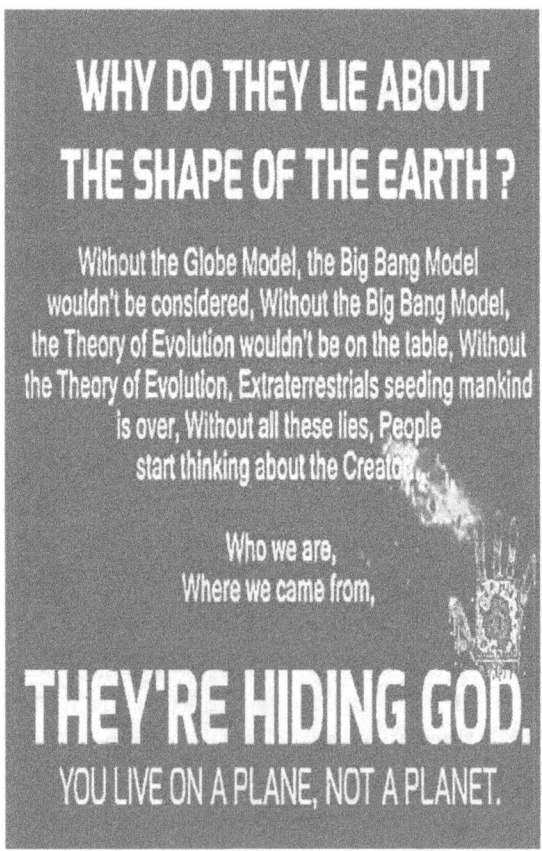

After the film premier, Nathan's entourage retreated to the family ranch a few hours' drive away. Dr. Thompsen was invited to stay in the RV, while Grandpa Benton selected the guest house. Myiah would get Nathan's bedroom, and he would sleep in his old tent by the Rancho.

Grandpa Benton drew laughs saying: "I'd rather be in the tent. Might be hard for me to be around so many people in a big or little house after all my time alone at sea. I'll have to work back up to it."

At the barbeque dinner outside in the Rancho, Nathan and Myiah sat with Great-grandma Tilly, who was cradling the rescue dog, Mighty Whitey, in her lap. She wore a cap that read 'A New Day at Ninety-Eight.'

"Let's sing a song together before we eat." Great-Grandma grinned. "How about 'Amazing Grace'?"

Nathan reached gently for her hand. "Did they ever teach you about the Flat Earth when you were in school, Grandma Tilly?"

The old lady lit up with a smile as broad as the moon. Then in a moment of true clarity, her eyes triggered bright. "Why yes, Nathan. Yes, they did! They taught us like in your movie. In those days, they even used Bible verses in the schoolhouse!"

Chapter Seventeen

Would you follow a Heliocentric lie?
An explosion made you? There's no Creator?
That you're an accident spinning in space?
Why follow lies of the devil?

After such a whirlwind, it was comforting to be back on the Ranch in Virginia. Russ and Sue enjoyed hosting the family and friends. Only his dad, Sam and ninety-seven-year-old, Grandma Tilly stayed on for a bit.

Everyone else had jobs and schools and responsibilities of life to get back to.

"The guesthouse treating you okay, Pop? Would you like to move into the house with the rest of us?"

"Aww, Son, it's fine. It's just a blessing to be together at our age." He smiled.

"Or at any age!' Grandma emphasized.

His father seemed reluctant to head home to an empty cottage on the Atlantic. No doubt due to so many memories; He mentioned calling out his wife's name a few times.

Still though, in a few days he planned to sail the Juggernaut back up the coast.

Meanwhile, they enjoyed studying the Bible with his father in the evenings. Dad was re-learning so much, surprised at their lay knowledge of the Scriptures.

Late the next night, Russ shared a cup of tea with him. "Scripture says before the second coming, there will be some genetic tampering."

"That right?"

"Yes, sir." Russ opened a Bible to Genesis 6. "Says here the fallen angels came into the daughters of men. I believe their union created the race of giants mentioned in verse four."

"That so?"

"Russ and I have come to believe that was the real reason God sent the flood—for Noah to preserve the pure bloodline. When analyzing the Tablet we discovered, it lined up with new DNA readings from the Dead Sea Scrolls."

"Woah. Discovered in the Qumran Caves in Israel, right?"

"That's right, in 1947. They overlook the Dead Sea in Israel."

Russ nodded. "The Nephilim giants were also discovered in the scrolls. Additional historical texts, such as the Book of Enoch from Ethiopia, and Jasher give the same accounts."

"Wow. Why are they so hell bent on keeping all of this a secret?" His father was a sailor . . . his vernacular could've been worse.

"It's like the truth behind the pharmakeia deception. They will spin their lies until everyone is drinking the tainted Kool-Aid. Plus, if the sons of the fallen angels are giants, it will be harder to explain the aliens from outer space."

"Or that we are not spinning in a vast cosmos at millions of miles per hour." His dad was catching on.

"Exactly."

There was one more piece of unfinished business between the two—a father and son on the mend.

"Listen, Son, there's something I want to ask of you."

"What, Dad?"

"I need to ask you for forgiveness…for my being so emotionally unavailable to you over the years."

"You came home most nights, even if you were usually late."

"Can you forgive me for physically abandoning you and family, too? And for not guiding you enough while growing up?"

The two sat reflecting for a time. Finally, Russ spoke first. "Of course, I forgive you, Dad. The Bible says that when we don't forgive someone, the Lord won't forgive us, but I forgive you because I love you."

"I love you too, Son." Tears welled-up in both men's eyes.

"You know, at the end of the day, you were a lot better Dad than most. I'm just thankful to God for you being here now."

On these cool evenings, Sue headed out to her studio where she exercised and painted when the mood struck. Late one night, the land line rang. She answered, happy to hear her daughter's voice.

"Mom, I'm going to be thirty in a couple of years. When did you and Dad start thinking about having kids?"

"Well, I'd recommend being married for a while first."

"Think I've fallen in love with professor Thompsen." Gwen filled her Mom in. . .

Hearing her sweet girl was smitten with her professor friend gave Sue's heart joy! The devil often tried to make her believe it would never happen for Gwen. But she had been devoted in prayer for God to send her a faithful man. "Love takes patience, sweetie."

"I know, I know. Great-grandma told me to take it slow, too, but . . ."

"I'm so happy for you, dear. Dad and I really do like him. He's definitely a keeper."

"Oh, Mom, I so agree!"

Traveling back to the west coast, Nathan loved having Myiah beside him on the plane ride home. They chatted about the future. He asked her on a bike ride to Griffith Park soon. There was a small lake on the way in the shape of a heart.

He told how she might enjoy exploring the Observatory to view the sacred heavens. He wanted to share his plans to transfer from U.C.L.A. to a faithful university and hoped she might do the same. He would wait to tell her at the heart lake.

He dropped a hint. "Dr. Thompsen mentioned receiving a teaching offer from a College on the East Coast, closer to Gwen." With Great-grandma Tilly now living with his parents, he couldn't justify staying at such a secular campus.

"Considering taking some time off from school to promote the documentary and finish my book." He shared, stepping off plane at LAX.

"Smart idea." Myiah held his hand. "A hot topic now."

Little did Nathan know an encounter was coming right up that would embolden his faith and give him the opportunity to share the Gospel.

Outside the airport baggage area, Nathan noticed a man sitting on the floor, propped up against a wall, wearing a T-shirt that read, I'm an Atheist—just ask.

"Stand by, Myiah, will you?"

"Of course. You go ahead. I'm fine."

He approached the atheist. "You don't believe in God?"

"Why should I?" The man glanced Nathan's way. "I like guilting Christians for money."

Nathan pondered whether to give a verbal response, then simply smiled and handed him a leaflet titled:

The Greatest of All!

"The greatest man in History had no servants, yet they called Him Master. Had no degree, yet they called Him Teacher. Had no medicines, yet they called Him Healer. He had no army, yet kings feared Him. He won no military battles, yet He conquered the world.

"He committed no crime, yet they crucified Him. He was buried in a tomb, but the grave could not hold Him, for He lives yet today. His name is Jesus."

What a surprise! The haggard looking man read the track aloud. "Haven't seen this one before." He nodded. "I've been homeless for a while. Not many people will stop and talk with me."

With his new boldness, Nathan smiled. "Ever wonder why someone should believe in God?"

" 'Bout every day."

"Well, here's my answer. I'd rather live my life believing in God and serving Him, and find out at the end I was right, than not believing in Him and not serve Hin, and discover I was wrong. It's too late then!

"There's no shame in His name! I believe in Jesus Christ. He said if we deny Him in front of our friends, He'll deny us in front of His Father. It's in the Bible; Matthew 10:33-35. I've paraphrased."

Nathan kneeled next to the man and spoke in a whisper. "You know it says that God sent His only Son, Jesus, to die for your sins."

"Yeah, yeah—I know all that—no drinking, drugs, lying, stealing, cheating, immoral sex, and all the rest. Too many rules, man."

"So, may I assume you'd fall on that list?"

"Assume whatever you want. Isn't everyone on it—from stealing a cookie as a kid? And you Christians say all you gotta do is raise your hand and say I believe, right?"

"Not exactly."

"Well, you go ahead and tell me then. What does someone need to do?"

"In Acts 2:38, Peter says we need to repent and turn from doing those sins. We need to be baptized in the name of Jesus, and we'll receive the gift of the Holy Spirit.

"Jesus Himself says in Mark 16 that he who believes and is baptized shall be saved, but he who does not believe shall be damned."

"Damned, huh? Like damned to Hell?"

"That's exactly right. Hell's a real place, you know. It's under the earth, not *in* the earth."

"So you have to be dunked or you're damned? What if I got baptized as a baby?" The homeless man made his way to his feet.

Nathan remained kneeling.

"It means when you are old enough to choose for yourself."

"Does your Bible say that?"

"It says that being fully immersed in water drowns all the demons of sin, then in the name of Jesus, it says you receive the gift of the Holy Spirit. You're born again!"

"Tell you what." The man poked a finger at Nathan. "I like you, so come on." Nathan stood. "I'm gonna let you and your pretty lady friend buy me lunch at the diner across the street, and you can go on about it."

"Alright." Nathan chuckled. "That sounds like a deal. I'm going to tell you something big. He's coming on the clouds, and everyone will see Him! And I believe He's coming soon."

Gazing up at the sky on his way to the diner, Myiah on his arm, he prayed a silent prayer.

"Father, let me never be ashamed. I believe in Your Son, Jesus Christ. Thank you, Jesus, for all You've given us. For being my best friend. Help me to share Your truth and love with everyone I meet Lord. Until that day when every eye will see You coming through those heavenly clouds in Glory!

Over Two Hundred Verses on Flat Earth—My Top 10:

"And God made two great lights; the greater light to rule the day (the sun) and the lesser light to rule the night (the moon) he made the stars also. God set them "IN" the firmament of the heaven to give light upon the earth." Genesis 1: 16-17

"He set the earth on its foundations so it should never be moved." Psalm 104:5

"He shall have dominion from sea to sea, and from the river unto the ends of the earth." Psalm 72:8

"It is He that sitteth upon the circle of the earth, and the inhabitants thereof are as grasshoppers. He stretches out the heavens like a curtain, and spreads them out like a tent to dwell in." Isaiah 40:22

"The earth takes shape like clay pressed beneath a seal..." Job 38:14

"And the servants of the Lorde lye in tentes upon the Flatte Earthe..." II Samuel 11:11 - KJV, dated: 1611

"So the Lord scattered them abroad from thence upon the face of all the earth." Genesis 11:8

"And He will gather the scattered people of Judah from the four corners of the earth." Isaiah 11:12

"Tremble before Him, all the earth; Indeed, the world is firmly established, it will not be moved." 1 Chronicles 16:30

"Behold, He is coming with the clouds, and every eye will see Him, even those who pierced Him; and all the tribes of the earth will mourn over Him. So it is to be. Amen." Rev. 1:7

Post Script

When my 'Biblical Earth' eyes were opened—
The Author's Account

Someone once asked me, "When were you given this understanding of the level earth shape?" At a younger age, I was so misled by science; raised in a scientifically-minded family. We attended church regularly and believed in a creator God.

However, they promoted a Big Bang Theory coexisting with the Bible. That we are on a speck of dust rotating in a vast universe, in a heliocentric solar system, spinning around in the Milky Way Galaxy. It sounded like a candy bar. But I still played along, spinning the model globe in our first-grade classroom, laughing along like all the rest.

Yet, deep down something within me told me a different story. In the Bay Area, we frequented the planetariums with school classes annually. Planetariums in the shape of a dome where the stars rotated above in a set pattern, predictable for eons—the North Star, Polaris, always fixed at the center.

That seemed illogical on a spinning rotating earth shooting through the universe at over a million miles per hour.

Later, with college astronomy classes, I knew the constellation names and gazed at the stars many nights.

Always, they were comforting, predictable, seeming to be close by.

Then, when my older brother, Daniel, was hired at the Lawrence Hall of Science Planetarium, I would accompany him to assist with presentations on occasion.

It felt empowering behind the controls of the tall projector. As a senior mathematics student, at the University of California in Berkeley, my brother Daniel was filled with knowledge, wonder, and questions.

There was a time in my teens, when my professor father, took a sabbatical, with the family traveling in Europe for a year. Mostly low-budget camping in our VW Van.

While visiting the Vatican, at age of fifteen, I confronted a priest in the lobby giving the tour. There was an enormous globe model of the round earth in the front lobby covered with signs of the Zodiac!

In front of our tour group, I wondered why the Vatican would prominently display signs used in divining horoscopes, used for pagan rituals—witchcraft!

The priest's answer was telling. "It's a big part of the church. Our church history." When I pressed him for further details, he became angry: *"Move on!"* The Italian accent was right out of a Godfather film.

My first memory of such things was as a four-year-old. Gazing up nightly in the Minnesota summer, we watched for the Russian Sputnik craft nightly. The first in space. During that Cold War, we considered the unthinkable.

Would the astronauts drop an atomic bomb on us from space? "Was this not for programming? To instill fear?

Then coincidentally, that same summer, the original black and white movie, *The Day the Earth Stood Still*, aired on TV.

In the film, an ambassador from a highly advanced alien race comes to earth to monitor earthlings after the development of the nuclear bomb.

They are to halt Planet Earth until there is a one world governing body established, for worldwide control and oversight. Sounds like the Antichrist in the *Book of Revelation*, bringing a false peace during the Tribulation.

Even later, as a young adult, I fell into the Hollywood snare with movies such as *Close Encounters of the Third Kind, ET the Extraterrestrial, Alien,* and TV shows such as *Star Trek.*

And let's not forget that at the start of every Universal film, a gargantuan spinning globe becomes larger and larger, until it dominates the entire screen.

Late at night, in my middle years, I would listen to talk show radio host Art Bell, spinning yarns into the wee hours.

Many of the guests, such as John Lear, or Bob Lazar, would discuss the U.S. secret base at Area 51, north of Las Vegas. Convinced they were housing aliens and reverse engineering high tech alien craft that were downed in mishaps, since the Rowell Incident in New Mexico in 1949. After all, the CIA was formed that year, as a result.

Only later, did I realize that all of this was mass deception, perhaps the world's biggest lie . . . a Masonic globe model.

At the turn of the century, after witnessing a project blue-beam demonstration near Area 51, I came to believe a deep black-op programs existed. They spread alien deceptions for domination and control, with a demonic transhuman agenda, and dare I state this? —for depopulation.

Finally, one of my stellar nephews reached out with several NASA frauds and faked videos. A graphic designer himself, knowing all too well the CGI—Computer Graphic Image hoaxes. Earlier, it was reported that NASA had hired artists to paint the planets.

There were fraudulent photos, presumably from space, of planet earth and much more. Faux spacewalks, done in underwater tanks that gave a myriad of clues, such as bubbles emitting from the astronauts' suits, and reflections of cameramen in their helmets.

Earlier, another relative of mine worked on the optics to repair the Hubble Telescope; designed to gaze billions of years into the past through deep space. His Tinsley company was awarded a lucrative government contract.

Enlarged photos of deep space were given to family one holiday. "All CGI fakes," my nephew reported, while examining some of the first released photos.

But I still hung on to a spinning globe. . .

The following week, my globe world was smashed after meeting author, Nathan Roberts, in Clarkesville, Georgia. Nathan is the author of *The Doctrine of the Shape of the Earth, a* comprehensive Biblical perspective.

While traveling in our RV at the time, my wife and I had stopped at a grocery store and were immediately drawn into a conversation over the face masks being mandated for entry.

Nathan was challenging the store manager over the masks, saying there were no laws in force on the wearing of them. He was right. Not to mention the health risks. He and his young daughter were allowed to shop without the masks.

My wife and I caught wind and joined them in this pursuit.

After shopping, Nathan and his daughter toured our modest RV. My wife and I had named it *Daisy* after her summer camp nickname one year as a youth.

When Elizabeth asked his daughter her name, she replied, 'Daisy!' A fortuitous moment for sure, leading to his sharing the Flat Earth Biblical Doctrine with us. He mentioned so many Scriptures that aligned with it.

We promised to read his book and look into the matter further.

As he waved goodbye from the grocery store parking lot, Nathan turned back with a clear message. It pierces our hearts even today: ***Remember, real Christians want the truth!***

After this chance encounter, it opened my eyes to see the creation in a new light. If the Bible is true, how could it say that the earth is stationery and immovable over thirty times? Nowhere does it say that the earth is a spinning round globe.

Have you considered Scripture is inerrant? God's word always proving itself infallible from the beginning? If you do, consider '*The fear of the Lord is the beginning of wisdom*,' as Solomon wrote in the Proverbs.

The NASA founder, Verner Von Braun, a former Nazi, took this fear to the grave. He had been recruited by the Masonic Illuminati to form and head NASA. They soon discovered their rockets could not penetrate the firmament.

On his tombstone are the words he asked to be engraved: ***"The Heavens declare the glory of God, and the firmament sheweth His handiwork"*** *Psalms 19:1*

Then while traveling back through Carpinteria, California one evening around dusk, we noticed a line of cars pulled to the side of the road overlooking the Pacific Ocean. People were outside their vehicles staring up into the sky.

Our older son, riding in the backseat, turned and spied a fast-moving object over the ocean. We stopped our own vehicle to have a look ourselves. Was it a UFO?

A young man standing nearby explained it was one of Elon Musk's Space X launches from Vandenberg Air Force base.

We wondered why the rocket was tracking at such an angle if it was supposed to be heading into space? Why are rockets never launched straight into the sky? We soon had our answer. The rocket suddenly began sliding further sideways after striking the firmament!

Vapor trails of water seemed to appear spreading out over the sky in a colorful mist. As you may recall, I write about the experience in the second chapter of this book, from the characters' perspectives.

So, there is the observable. Over the years in music, in business and now as a musical missionary, I have been blessed to travel the earth, not a globe.

In retrospect, everything does align with scripture. In Genesis you will find the Lord God spoke all of creation into existence; *"And God said, let there be light."*

I believe our Creator is increasingly revealing the truth of His enclosed stationary earth to believers and non-believers alike. Why? I believe it is important to Him. Many are finding faith and peace in this truth. "I feel closer to Him." My wife wisely said.

For me, I've been blessed to see the Level Earth from above the earth aboard a Falcon. A jet at forty thousand feet, not the bird. But faith is sufficient. It outweighs any proof.

Anyone can view the level seas that expand beyond the horizon, or touch the outer wall, along the earth's edge as the heavenly firmament rises above. Walk to the top of a mountain and see for fifty miles; there's no curvature. Traveling worldwide and viewing a midnight sun and the Aurora Borealis in Norway, is simply the added blessing.

To me, it is clear there is a dome covering, a firmament, created by the one true God on the first day. The land masses surrounded by seas on a stationary Level Earth, held in place by a circular outer ice edge wall.

But what truly sealed the Level Earth in my heart, is the Word of God. That Scripture never lies. Try praying and meditating on the first page of the Bible. This is most certainly our Holy God's creation, and it is ALL for His Glory.

In His Service,
Eric Alan Soldal
"The heavens declare the Glory of God; All for His Glory!"

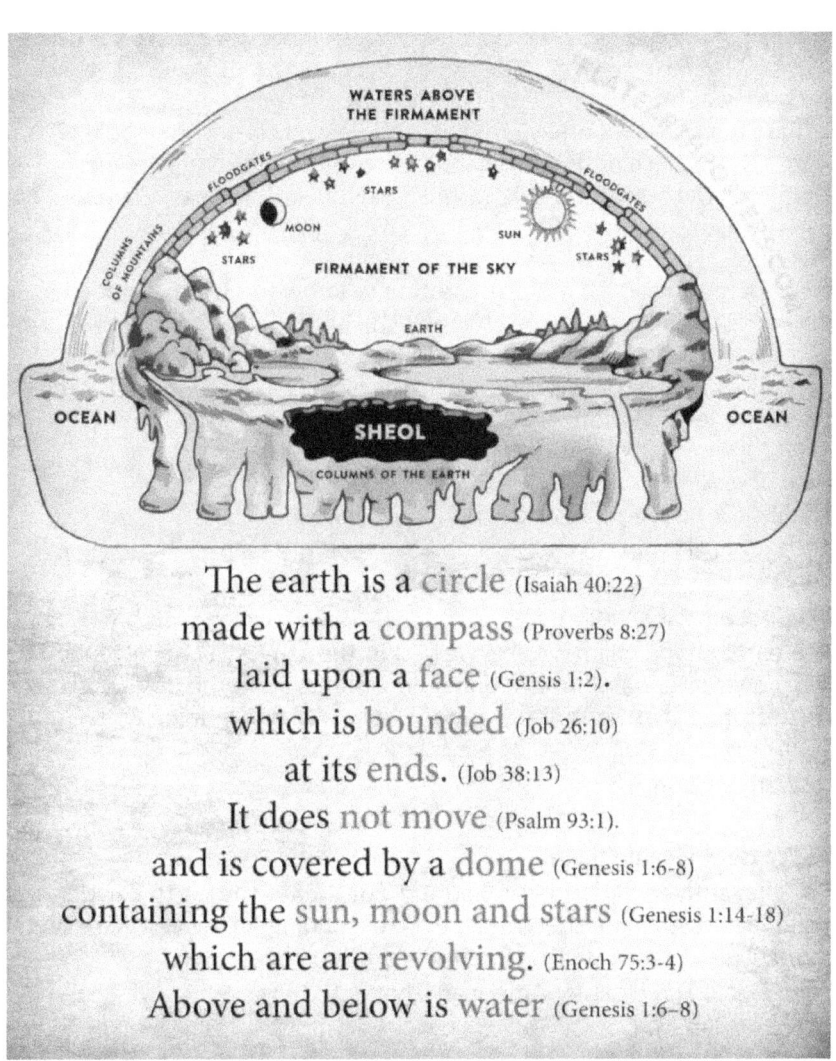

The earth is a circle (Isaiah 40:22)
made with a compass (Proverbs 8:27)
laid upon a face (Gensis 1:2).
which is bounded (Job 26:10)
at its ends. (Job 38:13)
It does not move (Psalm 93:1).
and is covered by a dome (Genesis 1:6-8)
containing the sun, moon and stars (Genesis 1:14-18)
which are are revolving. (Enoch 75:3-4)
Above and below is water (Genesis 1:6–8)

What Readers are Saying:

Such a great book!
A must read one. It's an eye opener and perfect for those people who want the truth. I'll definitely share this to my friends and families. Thanks to the author for this wonderful Novel! God bless, Claire H.

Riveting!
This is a must read for anyone wanting to know the truth about why they're covering up the true shape of the earth. It's written in the form of a Novel with a great storyline and includes Biblical and scientific backup. This book, with its powerful message, needs to spread across the entire level stationary earth! Alice L.

Nice one!
Thanks for helping spread the flat word, fellow Eric!
Eric Dubay, Flat Earth Author and Documentary Film Maker.

No Conspiracy Theory here-
The earth shape will never be viewed in the same way. Over forty-four U.S. government and international documents state the earth is flat and non-rotating. No conspiracy theory here. All in a griping 'can't put it down' exciting story!
Howard Wilson

We're on the same page!
You elegantly included how God did not create the earth for us as an insignificant spinning speck in an ever-expanding universe! We're on the same page as far as Biblical Cosmology goes!
Peggy Hall, The Healthy American Channel